# Wipeout

Doug tacked, then aimed his board directly at an incoming roller.

Suddenly he was upside down in midair. The bottom of his board was reaching for the sky, and the tip of his mast was aimed at the wave. A forward roll, one of the toughest maneuvers in boardsailing!

Frank was about to shout congratulations when Doug's mast seemed to come loose at the base. The loss of support threw Doug completely off balance.

A second wave caught the tip of Doug's sail. The mast seesawed wildly. Suddenly it cracked Doug across the forehead, and the board landed upside down in the surging water.

Joe stared, horror-struck. "His feet," he shouted to Frank. "They're caught in the foot straps! He's sure to drown!"

## The Hardy Boys Mystery Stories

#59   Night of the Werewolf
#60   Mystery of the Samurai Sword
#61   The Pentagon Spy
#62   The Apeman's Secret
#63   The Mummy Case
#64   Mystery of Smugglers Cove
#65   The Stone Idol
#66   The Vanishing Thieves
#67   The Outlaw's Silver
#68   Deadly Chase
#69   The Four-headed Dragon
#70   The Infinity Clue
#71   Track of the Zombie
#72   The Voodoo Plot
#73   The Billion Dollar Ransom
#74   Tic-Tac-Terror
#75   Trapped at Sea
#76   Game Plan for Disaster
#77   The Crimson Flame
#78   Cave-in!
#79   Sky Sabotage
#80   The Roaring River Mystery
#81   The Demon's Den
#82   The Blackwing Puzzle
#83   The Swamp Monster
#84   Revenge of the Desert Phantom
#85   The Skyfire Puzzle
#86   The Mystery of the Silver Star
#87   Program for Destruction
#88   Tricky Business
#89   The Sky Blue Frame
#90   Danger on the Diamond
#91   Shield of Fear
#92   The Shadow Killers
#93   The Serpent's Tooth Mystery
#94   Breakdown in Axeblade
#95   Danger on the Air
#96   Wipeout

**Available from MINSTREL Books**

THE HARDY BOYS® MYSTERY STORIES

**96**

# The HARDY BOYS®

## WIPEOUT

### FRANKLIN W. DIXON

PUBLISHED BY POCKET BOOKS

New York   London   Toronto   Sydney   Tokyo

A MINSTREL PAPERBACK *ORIGINAL*

 A Minstrel Book published by
POCKET BOOKS, a division of Simon & Schuster Inc.
1230 Avenue of the Americas, New York, NY 10020

Copyright © 1989 by Simon & Schuster Inc.
Cover artwork copyright © 1989 by Paul Bachem
Produced by Mega-Books of New York, Inc.

ISBN: 0-671-66306-2

First Minstrel Books printing June 1989

10 9 8 7 6 5 4 3 2 1

Printed in the U.S.A.

# Contents

1. Happy Landings!     1
2. The Villa Dombray     9
3. An Accident?     19
4. Fight!     28
5. A Deadly Logjam     40
6. Hot Stuff     51
7. Trouble in the Air     62
8. A Deadly Sport     72
9. The Hanging Bush     82
10. Last Chance     90
11. Out of the Deep     100
12. I Accuse . . .     110
13. At Bay at Last     117
14. Fight to the Finish     127
15. A Race for the Prize     136
16. The Villain Unmasked     145

# WIPEOUT

# 1 Happy Landings!

"The tops of those clouds look just like whitecaps —perfect surfing." Frank Hardy turned from the plane window back to the magazine he was reading, when a photo caught his eye. "Hey, Joe," he said. "Take a look at this."

There was no answer from the next seat. Frank leaned over. Behind the silvered sunglasses, his brother was sound asleep. Frank touched him on the arm.

Joe Hardy woke instantly. "Are we there yet?" He took off his sunglasses and looked around the cabin. The steady hum of the big jet's engines seemed to answer the question for him. "What time is it?"

"Almost eight o'clock, French time," said Frank. "Back in Bayport it's still the middle of the night."

Joe brushed back his blond hair, yawning. "It

*feels* like the middle of the night," he said. "Maybe my brain is still back in Bayport."

Frank grinned. "Don't worry. You usually forget to pack it," he joked. "I wanted to show you this."

Joe took the magazine. "*Wind and Wave?* Are you doing some background research?"

"Check the picture on page twenty-three."

Joe followed orders and looked at the photo. The guy on the sailboard wore a wild red-and-blue wet suit that matched his sail. The camera had caught him in the middle of a spectacular jump. A beach and the hills beyond it could be seen in the gap between the water and the bottom of the board. "Hey, that looks like Doug!"

Doug Newman was a top windsurfer, whose school in Bayport drew students from all over. Frank and Joe had both studied there the year before.

Joe read the photo caption aloud. " 'The place to be this month is Almanarre, in the south of France. The reason? The trials for the famed Almanarre Cup. Here champion rider Doug Newman trains for the meet he has aced two years in a row. Another win and the Almanarre Cup is his for keeps. Can he do it?' "

Frank nodded. "From what we've heard," he said, "that might be a good question. I wish I'd been home when Catherine called the first time."

2

Catherine Dombray was the French girl Doug was engaged to marry. The Hardys had met her a couple of months before at a party. She was tall and slender, with golden hair and a charming accent.

When Doug jokingly introduced the Hardys as "Bayport's famous detectives," she asked to hear about some of their cases. She was a good listener, and her intelligent questions had impressed the guys.

"I'd have recorded it, but I thought it was just a friendly call," Joe said. "Then Catherine started telling me how somebody's playing practical jokes on Doug. She thinks whoever it is wants Doug out of this meet."

"And we're supposed to find out who's pulling the pranks."

Joe nodded. "Sounds like a good reason to take a vacation in France."

A shiny cart stopped in the narrow aisle next to him. Joe and Frank each took a breakfast tray from the flight attendant.

Frank finished his scrambled eggs and toast quickly. "It may be a vacation if only jokes are involved," he said. "But if someone really tries to hurt Doug, it stops being funny."

Joe slipped his sunglasses back on. "Even if there's no mystery, we'll get to see Doug do his stuff. Front-row seats to a world-class sailboarding meet don't fall in your lap every day."

* * *

They stepped off the plane into warm sunshine. Doug was waiting for them just outside the customs barrier. He was wearing white shorts and an orange-and-green aloha shirt. The people around him kept glancing over, as if they were sure he was someone famous but couldn't figure out who.

"Hey, Frank! Joe!" Doug grabbed them by the arms. "How was your trip?"

"Great," Frank replied. "How are you doing?"

"Terrific, just terrific! I'm feeling really up for this meet."

"Oh?" said Joe. "No funny jokes?"

An embarrassed look crossed Doug's face. "I don't know why Catherine got so upset over nothing," he said. "It was silly to bring you all the way to France over a little run of bad luck."

He grinned. "Still, it's a treat to see you. Come on, my car's outside." He led them to a little white convertible and put the top down. Frank took the front seat while Joe climbed in back.

Doug started the engine, but instead of driving off, he turned to face the Hardys. "Maybe bringing you here wasn't so silly," he said. "Not for me, but . . ."

"Another problem?" Frank suggested.

Doug hesitated. "I guess so . . . Did Catherine tell you the place we're staying belongs to her?"

They shook their heads.

"Well, it does. The Villa Dombray. She inherited it last year from her uncle. Maybe you've

4

heard of him—Jacques Dombray, the famous sculptor?"

"I ran across his name somewhere," said Frank. "Didn't he design and engrave the Almanarre Cup?"

"Ten out of ten," Doug replied. "He loved windsurfing—bought a villa overlooking the bay just to watch everybody else whenever he wasn't out on the water himself. He was quite a guy."

"You knew him?" Joe asked.

"Sure. We kept running into each other at meets. Then he asked me to pose for a trophy he was sculpting. That was how I met Catherine."

He pulled out a pair of sunglasses and put them on. "Anyway," he continued, "when Jacques died last year, Catherine decided to try to keep the villa by turning it into an inn. She figured some of the windsurfers who knew her uncle would stay there when they're down this way and spread the word to others."

"That sounds like a good idea," said Frank.

"Catherine thought so," Doug said. "The place is booked for the whole season. Most of the big names at this meet are staying there . . ."

"I think I hear a 'but' coming," said Joe.

Doug nodded. *"But* . . . well, things have happened—funny sounds in the night, somebody messing with things in people's rooms. Accidents . . ."

"Any happen to you?" Frank remarked.

"I don't mean to me," Doug growled. "But last

week Fritz Meister, the slalom champ, was out on the terrace. He leaned against the railing and it broke, sending him into some bushes about eight feet down. He was lucky to get away with a few scratches."

Joe leaned forward. "Did anyone take a good look at the railing?" he asked.

"*I* did. And I don't know. It could have been a real accident—the wood was pretty old—or somebody could have helped it happen. Either way, it's bad news for Catherine."

He revved the engine angrily. "Look," he said, "boardsailors aren't any more superstitious than anybody else. But if word spreads that the Villa Dombray is bad luck, people will stay away— why take a chance?—and Catherine will be out of business before the end of the year." Doug looked at them. "I'm counting on you two guys to keep that from happening."

At the airport entrance, Doug turned sharply. "I'll take the corniche road back," he said. "That way you'll get a good look at the area."

A few moments later they were driving along a narrow, twisty road that clung to the side of a steep, brush-covered hill. Far, *far* below was the Mediterranean Sea. The surface was speckled with sailboards and small boats that left a cobweb of wakes on the dark blue water.

"It's like windsurfing heaven," Joe exclaimed. "I'm surprised you don't stay here forever."

"Stay?" replied Doug. "Here?"

6

The tires squealed as he jerked the little car around a tight curve. The road plunged down a steep slope. Doug hit the accelerator, and the convertible leapt ahead. "Sure," he said slowly, "I've thought about it. Thought . . ."

Another hairpin turn came, much too fast. Frank grabbed for the door as Doug slammed on the brakes. The car went into a wild skid. Suddenly they were sliding sideways down the road.

Doug spun the wheel one way, then the other. The car lurched, seemed about to flip over, then screeched back into its lane. An instant later a big diesel bus rounded the bend in front of them.

"I hate buses." Doug sounded as calm as if they were discussing the latest movie he had seen. "Always getting in the way."

They zoomed ahead. "You guys," Doug said, his words slurred. "Great guys. Good boardsailors . . . have talent . . . know how to work . . . but never great. Sorry, but . . . it's a gift. Know what the wind will do before the wind knows. Like detectives . . . Right?"

"Doug?" Frank said urgently. "Are you okay?"

"Me?" He blinked, then blinked again. "Never felt better. Why?"

The road crested a slope and started down again, clinging to the side of the hill. On the right was a wall of rock. On the left was thin air—and a long drop to the water.

"Not far now," said Doug. "Catherine . . . lunch . . ." He closed his eyes for an instant, then opened them wide. The car swerved toward the rocks, to straighten out at the last moment.

Frank put his hand on Doug's shoulder. "Hey, how about I drive?" he said. "You look tired."

"I'm . . . fine," Doug replied. The car lurched as he shrugged off Frank's hand. "No problem . . ."

His eyelids started to droop. "Just . . ."

Suddenly he slumped on the steering wheel. The little car sped up, veering toward the edge of the road.

Only a few scrawny bushes stood between them and a fatal plunge into the rocky surf far below.

# 2 The Villa Dombray

As the car lurched toward the edge of the cliff, Frank grabbed for the steering wheel. No luck— Doug was wedged against it. His legs, and the bulky transmission tunnel, kept Frank from reaching the brake pedal as well.

For a long moment the car began to slow down as the road leveled out. Then they were on another downward curve. Something—a pothole, a pebble—jolted the front wheels.

The car veered toward the rocky wall on the right. Just as the front bumper was about to graze the line of boulders, the car lurched again. This time there was nothing in front of them. Nothing except a clear blue sky and a sparkling blue sea two hundred feet below.

In the backseat, Joe struggled with his seat

9

belt. The latch seemed jammed, and his fingers fumbled desperately, pressing, pulling, and twisting. Just when he was sure that he would never get loose, the latch released itself. In a flash he slipped out of the shoulder harness and lunged forward.

He reached over the front seat, grabbed Doug's shoulders, and pulled him upright, away from the controls. In that same instant, Frank seized the wheel with one hand and the parking brake lever with the other.

The tires gave a long squeal of protest. Frank tugged harder on the brake lever. Gravel sprayed into the air, followed by a cloud of dust.

Suddenly it was over. The white convertible was sitting quietly by the side of the road. Frank turned off the engine, set the brake still harder, and climbed out. The front bumper of the car was sticking out over the edge of the cliff, and the left front wheel was less than an inch from the drop.

Joe joined him. "Whew," he said, looking over the edge, his face pale. "This one goes in our book of close calls."

"Too close," Frank replied. He wiped a hand over his sweaty forehead.

A sailboat was passing by just offshore. It looked no bigger than a kid's bathtub toy. Someone at the wheel noticed them and waved. They returned the wave, then stepped back carefully from the cliff.

"What about Doug?" asked Joe.

Frank took a deep breath and let it out slowly. "We'd better walk him around a little," he replied. "If we can't wake him up, we're going to have to hunt for a hospital."

They pulled their friend from the car and got his arms around their shoulders. He stumbled a lot as they marched him up and down. After a couple of minutes, he started to mumble protests.

Finally he straightened up and looked at the Hardys. "Somebody drugged me," he said in a groggy voice.

"It looks that way," Frank agreed. "Still . . . Have you been taking any medication?"

"Me? No way! Well, a hay fever tablet this morning. Something in Catherine's garden has been giving me fits. But those pills never did anything like that to me before."

Joe frowned. "Let's say you were drugged. Any idea who, or when?"

Doug shrugged. "At breakfast, I guess. It's served buffet-style. Anybody could have slipped something in my OJ while I was off getting seconds."

He glanced around. Suddenly he realized how close the car was to the edge of the cliff. His face turned white.

"This isn't funny," he said hoarsely. "We could have been killed!"

"We almost were," Frank replied. "Come on.

11

I'll take the wheel and you give me directions. The sooner we start our investigation, the better."

"Right," Joe added. "I'm beginning to take this case very personally."

Frank edged past two big motorcycles and stopped at the far end of the inn's gravel parking area. As he turned off the engine, Catherine Dombray came out onto the porch and waved, then started down the steps. When she noticed that Frank was behind the wheel instead of Doug, a look of worry crossed her face.

"Welcome to Almanarre and the Villa Dombray," she said as she came closer. "I am so glad you agreed to come. Doug, are you—"

He shot a glance at Joe and Frank, warning them to keep the near-accident to themselves. "I'm fine," he said. "I got a little sleepy on the way back, so Frank took over. How are you doing?"

She hesitated. "There was another . . . *incident* last night. I'll tell you about it later." She turned to the Hardys. "Are you very tired after your journey? Or would you like to look around?"

"You shouldn't miss the guided tour," Doug joked.

"Great," said Frank. He looked up curiously at the villa. It was bigger than he had imagined, three stories high, with rows of balconies outside the windows of the two upper stories. One corner of the red tile roof was being repaired. Metal scaffolding led up to it, and there were stacks of heavy clay tiles and other materials in the courtyard.

Catherine led them around to the front terrace. Joe let out an admiring whistle. The villa stood almost at the edge of a low cliff. Directly ahead was a wide, wind-whipped bay filled with brightly colored sailboards.

"My uncle loved this view," said Catherine. "So do I. If I have to give up this place, I don't know what I will do."

"Don't worry," Doug said. "With Frank and Joe Hardy on the case, all this nonsense will be over with in no time."

"I hope so." Her smile flickered. As she turned away, Frank noticed a hint of tears in her eyes.

She pointed to a narrow path that led down the side of the cliff. "There's a little cove down below," she explained. "You can swim whenever you like."

"Or launch a sailboard," Doug added. "That's one of the attractions of this place. It saves so much time. On weekends the traffic along Almanarre Beach gets fierce. Hey, why don't we try the waves after lunch? I can lend you boards."

"Terrific," Joe replied.

Frank smiled. "But maybe we should get a better idea of what's been going on first."

"Just what I was about to say," Joe said quickly.

"Sure," said Doug. "Let's get on with the tour,

then. Over there is the old barn. We use it as an equipment shed now. It's big enough for two or three of us to work on our boards at the same time or even stretch out a sail."

He unlocked the door to give them a look. Wildly colored boards and sail-wrapped masts were racked along two walls. At the far end, a workbench and a stack of sawhorses showed that this was more than just a storage room.

Doug carefully relocked the door. "We pay a lot of attention to security," he explained. "There's a ton of high-tech equipment in there, stuff that will be next year's latest improvements. We don't want anybody messing with it."

Joe asked, "Do you have the only key?"

"Oh, no," Doug replied, "that would make for too many hassles. Everybody who keeps his board here gets a key. That way they don't have to hunt for somebody to open the door every time they want to go out."

Joe glanced at Frank and made a face. Doug's "security" sounded about as secure as a safe made of aluminum foil. Doug noticed the look and started to redden.

Frank quickly changed the subject. "What's that building over there?" he asked Catherine.

"That was my uncle's studio, where he created his sculptures. I have kept it closed since he died, but if you would like to see . . ."

"Sure they would," said Doug. "So would I, to tell the truth."

14

"Of course." They walked across to the tightly shuttered building and Catherine pulled a ring of keys from her pocket. "I am not sure which one," she said. "It has been so long."

As she tried one key after another, she continued to talk, in a voice that grew more and more angry. "To start this inn was a dream of mine," she said. "A way of giving something to the sport my uncle loved so much. Somebody must hate me very much to want to spoil that dream."

"It might not—" Doug began.

She ignored him. "It is so senseless, so . . . *vicious.* Last night, while we were sleeping, someone broke into the villa. They took nothing, but they smashed three Chinese vases that had been in my family for many years. I found them this morning in little pieces. To steal a valuable antique for money, that I could understand, but to destroy it! Why?"

"There could be a lot of reasons," said Frank. "Once we find out more, maybe it will start to make sense."

"I hope so." She found the key she was looking for and swung the door open. "It's not knowing that is the worst."

The studio had the musty smell of a room that had been shut up a long time. Light flooded in from the big skylight in the roof, but the shuttered windows created a feeling of gloom. Half a dozen large sculptures, and many more smaller works, were scattered around the room. They

15

seemed to be waiting for Jacques Dombray to come back and finish them.

Hands in pockets, Frank wandered around the studio, looking at everything. At the back of the room, next to a big slanted drawing board, was a chest of drawers stuffed with papers. He tugged open the top drawer and pulled out a handful of leaflets for exhibitions and gallery shows. All featured Dombray's name, and most of them were sponsored by the Molitor Gallery in Paris or in a small resort town just up the coast from Almanarre.

Frank started to put back the notices. Then he saw, lower down in the drawer, a stack of drawings. He leafed through them. They were amazingly detailed. One, of a man's face, seemed strangely familiar. He had seen that face before, but where? Someplace odd, and not long ago. He stared at the drawing and tried to make the connection, but it didn't work.

Across the room, Doug and Catherine seemed to be arguing about something. Frank put the drawings back and closed the drawer, then moved closer.

"Sure, anybody could have done it," Doug was saying. "But who had the best reason? Ian has been out to get me for years. You know that. He's never managed to beat me on the water. Maybe he decided to try an easier way."

"He would *never* do something so sneaky and so dangerous," Catherine insisted.

"Even if it gave him a real chance to win the Almanarre Cup? Sure he would!"

Catherine shook her head fiercely. "I know him better than that. Yes, he'll do his best to beat you, but always fairly. To cheat would take everything away from winning."

Frank broke in. "Who is this Ian you're talking about?"

For a moment both Doug and Catherine looked surprised. It was as if they'd forgotten that Frank and Joe were there.

Then Doug said, "Ian Mitchell. He took second place at Almanarre the last two years. I think this year he's made up his mind to win, no matter what it takes."

"And me, I'm telling you this is not the Ian I know," Catherine said hotly.

Doug backed off. "Well, maybe not," he said. "But *somebody* drugged me this morning. And everybody knew I was driving to the airport. I call that attempted murder."

"This is terrible," said Catherine. "Terrible. And I am afraid there's worse to come." She looked around the studio sadly. "I'm almost glad that my uncle isn't here to see what's happening to the athletes he admired so."

The guys followed her outside and waited while she carefully locked the studio door. As they reached the corner of the villa, a man in jeans and a waiter's jacket called to Catherine.

"There's a sportswriter out at the front gate,"

17

he said. "He heard a rumor that Doug had an accident this morning. He wants to interview him about his chances of staying fit long enough to compete for the Cup this year."

Catherine's face hardened. "Again?" she exclaimed. "That's the third one this week. They're a flock of vultures. They *want* an accident to happen to Doug, just so they have something to write about!"

"Hey, they're not all like that," Doug said, leaning back against the scaffolding. "Some of my best friends are writers."

"That may be, but they're not welcome in my home!" She looked at the guy in the white jacket. "William, please tell this person to go away. I don't want him here—him *or* his friends."

As William turned to go, something, some flash of movement, caught Joe's eye. He glanced upward and gasped.

A heavy bundle of clay tiles was toppling from the scaffold near the roof. Turning in midair, it plummeted toward the terrace. Catherine, Doug, and Frank were directly underneath it. In another instant they would be crushed.

# 3 An Accident?

Joe dug his toes into the gravel, charging forward like a football fullback. Spreading his arms wide, he gathered in his three companions and drove them backward a dozen feet into a hedge.

As he fell on top of them, the tiles hit the ground, shattering with a loud crack. A thousand fragments flew like shrapnel.

Joe clapped his hand to the back of his neck. When he pulled it away, his hand was bloody.

"You're hurt!" Catherine scrambled to her feet and looked at his wound. "It's only a small cut," she said. "Come, I'll bandage it."

"Joe, look," Frank said urgently. "Up there, at that window!"

Joe looked where his brother was pointing. A man dressed in white was staring down from an open window right next to the scaffolding. He saw the Hardys looking at him and ducked back inside.

"Come on!" Joe sprinted for the door.

He found the stairs and took them three at a time. Frank was right behind him. At the first landing they paused long enough to glance both ways. The hall was empty. Had their quarry managed to get away?

As they ran up the next flight of stairs, a guy in white tennis shorts and shirt was starting down. He tried to brush past them, but Joe put out his arm and blocked the stairs.

"Who do you think you are?" the man blustered. "Get out of my way!"

"Not yet," said Frank. "We saw you at the window just now. Those tiles could have killed someone, you know."

"What's that got to do with me? I didn't drop them."

"Then who did?" Joe demanded. The cut on his neck was stinging and he felt as though he might have twisted his knee. "Come on, Charlie, talk!"

"My name isn't Charlie, it's Philip," the man replied. "And I won't talk because I've got nothing to say. I got back from a tennis game a few minutes ago. On my way upstairs to shower and change, I heard a crash. So I looked outside."

"You didn't see anyone?" asked Frank.

"Just you clowns, down in the bushes with Catherine and Doug. Now, would you mind letting me pass? I've got better things to do than stand around answering stupid questions."

20

Joe's fists tightened, but he caught a warning glance from his brother. What did they have on this guy, after all? Sure, he'd been at the window after the tiles fell. But there was nothing to show that he had pushed them down.

"Why were you going downstairs just now?" Frank asked in a quiet voice. "Didn't you say you were heading upstairs to shower and change?"

"So I changed my mind. Sue me. Hey, who are you guys, anyway? Where do you get off, asking all these questions?"

"I'm Frank Hardy, and that's my brother, Joe. Catherine asked us here because she's worried about all these, um, accidents."

"She ought to be," Philip sneered. "This place is jinxed. Now *if* you'll get out of my way . . ."

Joe stepped aside. As Philip went by, Joe wanted to help him down the stairs with a friendly boot, but he held himself back. "That guy's mouth is going to get him in trouble some-day," he remarked as they started up the stairs again.

"You've got it," Frank agreed. "But that doesn't mean he's the one we're looking for. Here, I think he was standing at this window."

Frank leaned out and looked down at the terrace. Then he pointed at the scaffold, a little to the left. "The tiles must have fallen from right about there."

He grabbed the metal support and stepped out onto the planks. Joe was close behind him. The platform was only about two feet wide, but a railing at waist height gave a feeling of safety. Three more bundles of the red clay tiles were stacked in the corner, near a ladder to the roof.

Joe bent down and pointed to several scratch marks in the wood. They led from the stack of tiles to a spot near the front edge. When the Hardys leaned over and looked down, the shattered bundle of tiles was directly beneath them.

"That's it, then," Joe said. He got down on his knees and felt the plank. "That's funny," he added, "it's soaking wet here. I wonder why?"

Frank gazed around. "I don't know—maybe they wet the tiles before they put them up. We'll have to ask Catherine."

"You know what else? Maybe big-mouth Philip is innocent after all. I don't see how he could have shoved the tiles off and gotten back inside before we looked up."

"It wouldn't have been easy," Frank replied. "But when we looked up, we didn't see anybody on the scaffold, did we? If Philip didn't do it, who did? And where did he go?"

Down below, a small van drove into the parking lot and two burly men in bright blue coveralls got out. They noticed the broken tiles at once, then looked up and saw the Hardys on the scaffold. One of them shook a fist at them, then the men hurried inside.

"I think we're about to meet the roofers," Frank said.

22

"That's amazing," said Joe with an admiring look. "You ought to be a detective!"

A few moments later the two men in coveralls were at the window. The one in the lead was wearing a dusty beret, and his friend had an unlit cigarette dangling from his lower lip.

Catherine was right behind. She quickly explained who Frank and Joe were and why they were on the scaffold. The workmen kept scowling. They didn't calm down until Catherine told them they wouldn't be held responsible for the broken tiles.

Joe and Frank climbed back inside. They were near the stairs when Frank turned back and asked the roofers if they used water in their work.

"No, m'sieu," the one in the beret said. "The tiles at the peak, that are set in mortar, we soak first. The others, no. There is no need."

"Oh," said Frank. "I see. Okay, thanks."

On their way down, the Hardys got their first real look at the interior of the villa. At the foot of the stairs was a wood-paneled hall hung with paintings. Wide doorways opened onto a big dining room on one side and an even bigger lounge on the other. Through the French windows at the end of the hall, they saw a view of the terrace and the sea beyond.

Joe glanced into the lounge and murmured, "Uh-oh."

Doug was in the middle of a hot argument with

23

Philip. About a dozen other people were standing around them, listening.

". . . can't pin it on me," Philip was saying. "I don't know how those tiles fell off the roof. But I know this—too many things have been happening around here. This place is just plain bad luck. Sooner or later somebody's going to get killed. Why wait around for it to happen? Why not get out now?"

Catherine, standing next to Frank, grabbed his arm. He had the feeling that, without his support, she might have slumped to the floor.

"The sooner *you* get out," Doug said, "the happier the rest of us will be. And don't try to kid me. If I'd agreed to endorse those tenth-rate sailboards you design, you wouldn't be talking so much about bad luck."

"Why would I want an endorsement from somebody who's over the hill? We'll all know who's tenth-rate and who isn't, before the week's over."

Doug's eyes narrowed. For a moment it looked as if he was going to throw a punch. Then his shoulders relaxed a fraction of an inch.

"So that's it," he said. "You figure all this talk about bad luck will rattle me before the meet and make me lose. Then no one will care what I think about your lousy boards."

Philip started to say something, but Doug just raised his voice and kept talking.

"But I'm not going to lose, no matter how much

24

you want me to. I'm going to win and retire the Cup. When I do, when the guys from all the boardsailing mags come around to talk to me, I'm going to tell them a few things. They'll hear about certain hotshot designers whose boards belong in a bathtub. And they'll get an earful about people who try to spook the entries in a major meet and affect the results, with talk about bad luck and jinxes."

"The bad luck's real," Philip said sullenly. "We all know that. The accidents are real, too. You don't need anybody else to spook you, Doug. You're spooked already, and we all know why."

He pointed his finger at Doug's chest. "You've lost your edge, Doug. You're past it. Finished. Your chances of winning the Almanarre Cup again this year are too small to be found with a microscope. Who knows? Maybe you like having all these accidents happen around here. They'll make a great excuse when you go down in flames!"

Once again Doug looked as if he was about to knock Philip to the floor. And once again he controlled his temper. "Sure, the accidents are real," he said. "But I don't think they're accidents. Somebody's behind them, and I'm starting to have a pretty good idea who that person is."

He looked around the room. The others all followed his eyes.

"Come on, Philip," Doug demanded, looking back at him, "clue us in. After I said no to endorsing your line of boards, who did you get to say yes? Who are you betting your business on to win the Cup this Saturday?"

With everybody looking at him, the designer turned red. "Who says I signed anybody?" he demanded. "When people see what my new boards can do, they'll be falling all over one another to endorse them."

Doug laughed. "Right. And if they try to ride one of them, they'll be falling over, period! Get serious, pal. Of course you signed somebody else, and we can all guess who. The same guy who'll do anything—*anything*—to win this meet."

He craned his neck and looked over the crowd. "And wouldn't you know it—here he is. Come on in, Ian. We were just talking about you."

A short, muscular guy with close-cropped blond hair and a rattail stood in the doorway. He was wearing bright red jams, a black sleeveless T-shirt, and an expression of fury. In his right hand was a shattered mast mount.

"I want to talk to *you*, Newman," he said in a loud voice. "You see this mount? It broke on me this morning, a mile and a half out into the bay. I had to paddle my board back."

"Tough," said Doug. "Maybe you ought to upgrade your gear. Trade it in for something a little more reliable. You'll be glad to know that whatever you slipped in my juice this morning worked just fine. It's not your fault that I'm not at the bottom of a cliff somewhere."

26

"I don't know what you're talking about," Ian replied angrily. "Don't try to change the subject. Somebody messed with my fitting—somebody who couldn't take the idea of being shown up for the has-been he is. Somebody named Doug Newman!"

Ian charged forward and shouldered his way through the circle. Doug squared off and raised his clenched fists, but Ian pulled back his weightlifter's arm, ready to hurl the heavy steel fitting right in Doug's face.

# 4 Fight!

The onlookers moved back out of the target zone. But Frank sprang forward, pulling Doug aside. At the same moment, Joe ran in front of Ian Mitchell and grabbed his wrist with both hands.

"Let's cool it a little, huh?" he said.

Ian swore at Joe, trying to wrestle his hand free. He was strong, but so was Joe, and Joe had better leverage. After a couple of moments, Ian stopped struggling and took a deep breath.

"Okay, guy," he said, "truce. But how about a few rounds of arm wrestling, one-arm-on-one?"

Joe grinned. "Sure, when I have the time."

"Who are you, anyway?"

"My name's Joe. Joe Hardy."

"No lie—Cathy's pet detective?"

"You could say that, I guess."

Ian held out the broken fitting. "Then how about detecting who messed up my mast mount?"

He raised his voice, staring hard-eyed across the room. "Not that I don't know the answer already."

"Ian, please." Catherine stepped forward and put her hand on his arm. "Don't make any more scenes. Aren't things bad enough already?"

Ian pointed at his rival. "They're going to get a lot worse if that one keeps making all these wild accusations," he said. "I don't have to dope his juice to win this meet, and he knows it."

"What about pushing a bunch of tiles off the roof?" asked Joe in a carefully neutral voice.

"Detecting, guy?" Ian said. "Okay, I'll play— when did this happen?"

Joe glanced at his watch. "Call it half an hour ago."

"About then, I was paddling my way in with a broken mast mount. There must have been five hundred people on the beach who saw me doing it. Lots of them thought it was funny. *I* didn't."

"Ian," Catherine pleaded.

"Look, I'm sorry I blew up, okay? And if Dougie wasn't in back of wrecking my board, I'm sorry I accused him. As for putting sleeping tablets in his tomato juice, it wasn't me, but I can imagine why somebody might want to do it."

"How did you know it was sleeping tablets?" asked Joe.

Ian shrugged. "How did I know it was tomato juice?" he returned. "I guessed. Big deal."

Doug surged forward. "You know it *wasn't* tomato juice," he shouted. "You were sitting right across from me!"

Ian shook his head in disbelief. "Listen, Mr. Numero Uno," he said, "this may come as a shock, but most of the world doesn't care what you have for breakfast. Unless it's one of those health-food messes you concoct—they're always good for a laugh."

"Ian!" said Catherine. "Doug! Please stop it, both of you!"

Frank stepped up. "Are you both sure you want everyone to hear what you're saying? This kind of thing isn't good publicity for anybody."

Doug seemed startled, and Ian glanced around the room, astonished to see so many listeners.

Joe noticed the guy in a waiter's uniform, whom Catherine had called William, come up and touch her on the shoulder. They whispered for a few moments, then William vanished.

Catherine raised her voice. "Listen, friends," she said, "lunch will be a little bit late today. A matter of technical problems—very boring, very upsetting. I know you understand. It happens all the time in windsurfing, right?"

"You bet!" someone called.

"But I'm hungry!" someone else shouted. The crowd laughed and cheered.

"Don't worry," said Catherine with a smile. "William is putting a snack out on the front terrace. If you will all—"

The stampede to the terrace had already begun. Catherine's smile faded as the room emptied, leaving her alone with Doug, Ian, Frank, and Joe.

"I have things to do now," she said, turning to the two rival boardsailors. "I hope you will both think before you argue again in public. If these fights do not stop, no one will want to stay here. You know what that means for me."

Joe was surprised to see Doug and Ian stare at their feet like little kids getting a scolding.

"Okay, Cathy," Ian said. Doug mumbled an agreement.

"Thank you," she said. "Now, there's fresh fruit and a wonderful goat cheese made by a farmer near here."

"With some help from his goats," Doug said. Ian laughed and punched him on the shoulder, and they went out the door to the terrace together.

Catherine watched them go. "When I first met them, they were good friends," she said. "Rivals, yes, but friends, too. It is sad when a friendship is lost, but to see it turn to hatred . . ."

She shook her head, then looked around at Frank and Joe. "Please," she said urgently, "find out who is doing these terrible things and stop them. Before it is too late for all of us."

\* \* \*

31

On the terrace, the Hardys put together plates of fruit, cheese, and bread, taking them to a table away from the others.

Joe took two bites of his peach, then put it down. "Well?" he said. "What do you think?"

"I think Catherine's right," Frank replied, spreading crumbly white goat cheese on a hunk of French bread. "This is a serious business, and it's getting more dangerous by the hour."

"Well, we've got two obvious suspects: Ian and that guy Philip," Joe continued.

"You left out another possibility," said Frank. He took a bite of bread and cheese, chewed it thoughtfully, and swallowed. "Hey, not bad. My compliments to the goat."

"Another possibility," Joe prompted.

"Uh-huh. Ian and Philip could be working together. Remember, Doug hinted that Philip might have talked Ian into endorsing his new line of sailboards. That would give *both* of them a motive to spoil Doug's chances."

Joe pounded his fist on the table. "It sure would," he said. "But what about Ian's broken mast mount?"

"Smokescreen," Frank explained. "If he's a victim, who'd suspect him of being behind it all?"

"Sure, it's obvious! And if one of them has an alibi for something, all it means is that the other one did it. Fantastic!"

Frank glanced around. No one seemed to be

paying any attention to them. "Remember, it's just a theory," he said, lowering his voice. "What we really need are some facts. I'd like to take another look around this place, without a guide this time."

"And without having to duck falling tiles," said Joe.

"I wonder if Catherine would give us the key to her uncle's studio," Frank continued. "I saw something there that's been nagging at me. Looking through a chest, I found a bunch of drawings in the top drawer. One of them was the face of a man that I'm sure I've seen somewhere before."

"Somebody you know?"

Frank shook his head. "Not exactly. More like . . . I don't know. Maybe it'll come to me. Meanwhile, why don't we split up? That way we can cover twice as much territory in the same time."

"Sure," said Joe. "And we'll meet at lunch to talk over whatever we've learned."

Joe put their plates away, then entered the villa. Frank sat for another few minutes, looking over the other guests at the villa and trying to fit names to those he had already met.

Finally he stood, wandering toward the equipment shed. If Ian's board really had been tampered with, that's where it must have happened.

The door was propped open, and a guy with shaggy blond hair was bent over, doing something to a purple-and-yellow board. Frank walked in quietly. Had he just discovered their saboteur?

As his body blocked the light from the door, the blond guy looked up. "Hello," he said. His accent was almost American, but not quite.

"Hi," said Frank.

"You must think I'm pretty silly to be doing this," the guy continued.

"No. What *are* you doing?"

"I'm parallel sanding the bottom with four-hundred-grit paper. They say this can add two-tenths of a kilometer per hour to the board's speed. Not much, huh? But even a few hundredths can make the difference between winning and losing."

"I didn't know," Frank admitted. "I haven't done that much windsurfing, and only for fun. My name's Frank, by the way."

"Olaf," the other said, putting out his hand. "I'm from Sweden. You're American, I think?"

"That's right." Frank shook Olaf's hand. "My brother Joe and I came over for the competition."

"You must be very eager to come so far. Not so long ago, only those who competed, and a few friends, would be at a meet. But the sport is changing very fast. Too fast, I think."

Frank leaned against a nearby sawhorse. "Oh?" he said. "How's that?"

"Money," Olaf replied. "When I began racing, we would pile four or five in a car, tie our boards on top, and drive in turns to the meet. Prize

34

money went to pay for gasoline and tolls. Everyone knew everyone, and if we fought hard on the water, we were friends on shore."

He sighed. "No more. To be serious, you must fly to Japan, to the West Indies, to Australia. One camber-induced sail can cost as much as most boardsailors earn in a year on the water. Sponsors are everything, and they want only the biggest names. It's getting worse, too. I hear that a television company is planning to pay a lot of money to broadcast a few important meets. And it's the big names that make the meets important, right?"

Frank frowned thoughtfully. "So winning the Almanarre Cup is worth a lot of money and power."

"More than the prize itself." Olaf grinned. "I wouldn't mind winning myself. But I know there are four people, maybe five, who are usually better than I. That's why I'm sanding this board. With that, and a wind that is exactly right, and a few tiny mistakes by the others . . ."

Frank returned his grin. "Well, good luck," he said. Olaf picked up his sandpaper again.

Frank continued around the villa. In the parking lot, the two roofers were chatting with a bearded middle-aged man at the wheel of a black Mercedes. As Frank walked past, the one in the beret glared at him. Did they still blame him and Joe for the damaged tiles? The atmosphere at the villa was being poisoned by suspicion. The sooner he and Joe discovered who was responsible, the better.

Joe was feeling frustrated. He had just wandered through every hallway in the villa, poking his head in at every open door. All he had discovered was that the place had a lot of rooms.

At the end of the hall, French windows opened onto a tiny balcony. He stepped outside. The view was breathtaking. Out on the bay, a hundred or more sailboards jibed and tacked in every direction. The beach was crowded with sunbathers and windsurfing enthusiasts. Farther out, a big white cruise ship made its way eastward. It left a thin line of smoke across the sky.

He glanced around the grounds. To his surprise, the door of the studio was wide open. A moment later, he saw Catherine walk across the lawn in that direction. Would this be a good time to check out that drawing Frank had talked about? He hurried downstairs and across to the studio.

From the doorway, he saw Catherine at the far end of the huge room, deep in conversation with a bearded middle-aged man.

"I won't need it for very long," Catherine was saying. "With the guests I already have booked, I can repay you in the fall."

The man patted her shoulder. "My dear," he said, "I am not a banker, I am a friend. Of course you may have another loan. But I am afraid you must take some advice along with it."

"I know, Emil. You think I should give up."

"Yes. You are already in debt, no? And if all does not go well, you could even lose the villa. I have started to hear rumors that all is *not* going well. People talk of prowlers and accidents and guests who are deciding to leave. How long will these bookings you speak of last if these disturbing things go on?"

Catherine put her chin up. "I don't know. But I will not give up so easily. I've brought in two wonderful detectives to find out who is making the trouble. They've had a lot of successes, and I'm sure they'll put a stop to it."

Joe's ears burned. He made up his mind to do whatever it took to help Catherine keep her inn.

"So?" Emil said. He sounded skeptical. "Well, you know that I still would like to make this place into a museum for your uncle's work. He deserves to have a monument like that.

"Now that I am on the subject," he added, glancing around, "what was the great artist working on in those last months? Was he doing any engraving? Dombray prints bring a good price these days. And though my plant is very small, I have skilled workers who can print them as he would have liked."

"I don't know," Catherine confessed. "He became very secretive toward the end. I wasn't even allowed in here. At mealtimes I left a tray

37

outside the door and knocked. He wouldn't even open the door until he heard me walk away."

"Oh? How sad."

"The one thing I know he did," Catherine continued, "was some additional work on the Almanarre Cup. I know that because, after he died, the curator of the museum came to take the Cup back. I had to search a long time for the key."

"The Cup, eh?" Emil started toward the door, Catherine at his side. Joe stepped behind a big statue of a man with two children and stayed out of sight. "Well, that is not something I can show at the gallery. Not to sell, at least. A shame."

Catherine closed the door behind her. When Joe heard the click of the lock, he almost called after them. Then he saw the latch on the inside, under the knob. He could leave whenever he liked.

He strolled down the center of the room, studying the sculptures. They were interesting, but he couldn't imagine what they had to do with the case. The nighttime troublemakers weren't a bunch of statues, after all!

The chest of drawers was just where Frank had said. Joe opened the top drawer, leafing through the stack of papers casually, then with more care. Putting the papers on the floor, he emptied the second drawer, then the third. He was careful to keep the contents of each drawer separate.

Once the chest was empty, he began putting

the papers back. He gave every page at least a glance, and some he studied a long time. When the job was done, he straightened up and brushed the dust off his hands.

This was weird. The drawing of a man's face that Frank had described wasn't there—not in the top drawer, nor in any of the rest.

He'd seen lots of papers, of every sort. But every single drawing in the chest had vanished.

# 5 A Deadly Logjam

Joe stepped back, looking slowly around the shadowy studio. Maybe he'd misunderstood Frank. The drawings could be somewhere else. But the longer he looked, the more he was sure that he hadn't made a mistake. That was the chest Frank had described, and the drawings weren't there.

He gazed at the ceiling, thinking hard. How could they vanish? According to Catherine, the studio had been locked since her uncle's death. He'd seen her relock the door after their visit.

Before he came up with an answer, his eyes froze on the huge skylight in the roof. Something blocked the light down toward the bottom—something round, the size and shape of a head.

Suddenly, the object disappeared. An instant later he heard a muffled crash and a faint cry. Someone had been spying through the skylight!

His dash for the front door beat his personal

best, but the lock stuck. By the time he managed to get out, it was too late. No one was in sight.

He walked slowly to the back of the studio, staring at the ground. At the rear, a stack of logs waiting to be split for firewood reached nearly to the top of the wall. A dozen logs lay scattered on the ground. He stared at one of them. It was mossy on one side, and some of the moss had been scraped off very recently.

Okay—the eavesdropper had stood on the log pile to look into the studio. Joe decided to check it out. He clambered to the top of the stack and stood up. By holding the rain gutter, he easily reached the level of the skylight.

Peering in, Joe could see the whole room—including Catherine as she opened the door and walked in. She glanced up, and her eyes seemed to meet his. Joe heard her scream as clearly as if she'd been standing next to him. He jumped back, and the stack of logs shifted under his feet.

With a rumble like distant thunder, the log pile began to collapse. Joe clutched the metal rain gutter and tried to do a quick chin-up. If he got in the way of those logs, he'd be lucky to get away with nothing worse than a broken leg.

As suddenly as it started, the avalanche of logs stopped. Joe waited a moment, then hung at arm's length and stretched his feet downward. His toes touched something that felt solid. But was it really? If he put his weight down, would he start another log slide?

The edge of the gutter was cutting into his fingers. He didn't have much choice—in a few seconds he was going to have to let go. Joe glanced down, shifted his toes to a more reliable-looking location, and dropped.

For one awful moment the log pile began to slide again. Then it stopped. Joe didn't wait to see how long. He leapt the remaining six feet to the ground and did a perfect tuck and roll.

"Joe Hardy! What . . . !"

He looked up from the ground. "Hi, Catherine."

"What were you doing up there? You really scared me!"

As he scrambled to his feet, Joe decided not to mention that he had been inside the studio earlier.

"Er, I surprised somebody on top of the log pile and scared him away," he said, perfectly truthfully. "After he ran off, I climbed up to see what he had been up to. I mean—"

"I understand," Catherine said with a grave smile. "What do you have in your hand?"

"Huh?" Joe looked down. Clutched in his left hand was a white terry-cloth wristband, the kind tennis players wear to keep slippery sweat off their hands. Where had it come from? It must have been in the rain gutter—he'd grabbed it unknowingly when he started to fall.

"I'm not positive," he said, "but I think I saw

42

something just like this earlier today. On the wrist of that guy named Philip."

"Philip Barstow?" Catherine looked startled. "I just passed him on his way inside."

"Oh? I think I'd like a little talk with him."

"And I should get back to my work," Catherine replied. "Lunch will be ready soon, and I have to make sure that everything is as it ought to be."

Joe found Frank in the lounge and quickly filled him in. Together they found Philip sitting on the terrace with a newspaper in front of his face. They took the chairs on either side of him and Joe tossed the wristband on the table.

"You lost this," he said.

The board designer looked up. "I don't know what you're talking about. Why don't you guys leave me alone?"

"You didn't ask Joe where he found it," said Frank. "Maybe because you already know?"

Philip stared straight ahead, tight-lipped.

Joe leaned back and peered under the table. "You know, you got moss stains on your tennis shoes climbing those logs," he remarked. "Hard to get out, moss stains."

Philip looked down. "It must be grass," he said.

Frank shook his head and said, "I hate to think what will happen to your business when all the top windsurfers in the world find out that you've been pulling these dirty tricks."

43

"Wait a minute," Philip said, staring at him, then at Joe. "I didn't pull any dirty tricks!"

Joe picked up the wristband and tossed it in the air a few times.

Philip watched as if hypnotized. Suddenly he said, "Okay, okay! I saw Catherine and some old guy going into the studio, and I climbed up on the log pile to listen. I thought maybe I'd learn something useful."

"Something you could use for blackmail?"

"I didn't say that—I hoped for something to stop Doug Newman from bad-mouthing my new boards. A lot of good it did me—I nearly broke my neck."

"What about the rest?" Frank demanded. "The falling tiles? The dope in Doug's juice?"

"I don't know a thing about any of that stuff!" Philip looked from one to the other. "I swear I don't! Look, you've got to believe me!"

Frank's eyes met Joe's. Frank raised one eyebrow, and Joe nodded. It didn't really matter whether they believed the designer or not. What counted was that they didn't have any real evidence against him.

Joe tossed Philip the wristband. "Next time, remember what they say about curiosity and cats."

Philip opened his mouth to reply, but at that moment the gong sounded for lunch. He sprang up and hurried away. The Hardys looked at each other and started to laugh.

44

"Hey, you guys," Doug called from the doorway, "come on. Aren't you hungry?"

After lunch, Doug followed Joe and Frank out onto the terrace again. The sky was a brilliant blue, with just enough fluffy white clouds to make the color look deeper. The sea was calm, and the air was so still that not a leaf seemed to move.

Most people would have called it a beautiful day, but Doug scowled. "Just my luck," he groaned. "I was hoping for some heavy-duty training time this afternoon. Instead I'm going to be on the beach with everybody else, waiting for wind. You guys want to stand around with me?"

Joe started to speak, but Frank quickly said, "Not just now, Doug. I think we'll stay here and catch some rays. See you later?"

"Sure. I'd better mount a light-air sail."

He went off toward the equipment shed. Joe looked at his brother and said, "Catch some rays? What are you talking about?"

"Why not? And maybe we can catch a little private conference time, too, while we're at it."

They settled in a couple of chairs near the edge of the terrace, closed their eyes, and basked in the sunlight for a few minutes. Then Frank said, "What do you say we ask ourselves a few questions?"

This was something Frank had picked up from their father. Fenton Hardy, a former member of the New York City Police Department, was now a

45

well-known private eye. Recognizing the detective streak in his sons, he'd begun teaching them the tricks of the trade.

"When you begin an investigation," he'd explained, "all you have is questions—lots of them. Try asking *yourself* the questions first. Then move on to other people. Sooner or later, you'll hit the right person with the right question at the right time. Then you'll start getting answers."

"Okay," said Frank now. "Who doped Doug's juice? Did they know he'd be on a dangerous road? Did they know he was bringing us from the airport?"

Joe frowned. "Ian Mitchell knew who we were this morning. If he knew, others could have, too."

"Why were the antique vases smashed? To scare Catherine? To make everybody nervous? To send a message to someone that we don't know how to translate?"

"Or was it plain meanness?" Joe contributed.

"Uh-huh." Frank paused to think. "Who is the target of all these incidents? Doug himself? A lot of things seem to be happening to him. But then who tampered with Ian's board, and why?"

Joe sat up. "Don't forget people hearing strange noises at night and finding the things in their rooms moved around."

"Somebody doesn't like windsurfers and wants to scare them away?" Frank said, grinning.

"Or maybe somebody owns an inn down the road and wants their business?"

46

"We're getting a little silly," Frank warned. "What about the falling tiles? Were they meant to hit us or miss us?"

"There were four targets—you, me, Doug, and Catherine. Those tiles could have been meant for any—or all—of us." Joe frowned. "Since we only just got here, it wouldn't be very fair to aim at us."

"I'll tell the bad guys you said so, once we catch up with them. Or him. Or her. Let's see, what else?"

"That's enough for a start," Joe said. This guessing game had always bugged him. He liked answers a lot better than questions.

Frank looked at him and reached over to touch Joe's forehead. "The sun's overheating your brain," he said. "Maybe you're thinking too hard. How about a quick, cooling swim?"

"You're on," Joe said, springing to his feet. "Last one in goes back for the towels!"

At dinner Catherine beckoned them over to sit at her table. The other seats were already filled. Doug was on Catherine's left, and Ian Mitchell was just across from her. Joe sat between Ian and a dark-haired man who introduced himself as Khaled. Frank took the chair next to Philip Barstow, who looked up, grunted, and went back to studying his plate.

"Hey, there," someone said on Frank's other

side. It was Olaf, the windsurfer he had met earlier in the day.

Frank smiled. "How's the sanding?"

"Tiring." The Swede sighed. "Very tiring."

Before Frank could reply, Catherine touched his arm. "I wanted you near me," she said, "so I can explain our dinner tonight. It is a dish from North Africa called *couscous*."

Ian sang, "With a couscous here, and a couscous there, here a cous, there a cous, everywhere a couscous . . ."

"Oh, be quiet," Catherine said with a smile. She turned back to Joe and Frank. "Do you know couscous at all?"

They shook their heads.

"Ah." She began to serve them from the bowls on the table. "It's a sort of tiny pasta," she said, "steamed over vegetables. These are the vegetables, which go on top. Sometimes—like tonight —we eat couscous with meat as well."

"You left out the best part," Khaled said.

"Yes. Khaled is our local expert on couscous," she added, and pointed to a small bowl of red sauce speckled with tiny yellow seeds. "This is called *harissa*."

"Otherwise known as volcano in a bottle," Ian joked. "Ever eat nachos with jalapeños?"

"Sure," Joe replied. "We love them."

"Well, next to harissa, jalapeños are about as spicy as vanilla fudge."

"Hot, huh?"

"Tell me about it," Ian said with a knowing grin.

"Harissa is piquant," Catherine admitted, "but one uses only a tiny amount to bring out the flavor of the couscous. And you don't have to use it at all if you don't want to."

Doug had been listening with a doubtful expression on his face. Now he said, "Take my advice and stay away from that stuff. You have to be some kind of idiot, deliberately putting poison in what you eat."

Frank noticed that Doug's plate contained what looked like spaghetti with tomato sauce. "You don't like couscous?" he asked.

"It's okay, but I'd rather have something really healthy. Take my spaghetti sauce—it's got wheat germ, brewer's yeast, powdered milk whey, and oil of garlic, all proven to be good for you, plus a couple of secret ingredients. And I only eat it with whole wheat spaghetti."

Frank kept his face blank, but he couldn't help thinking that it sounded pretty awful.

Ian seemed to agree. He said, "Doug is the head of the local chapter of Nuts and Flakes."

"Laugh all you like, yo-yo," Doug retorted. "Eating healthy is an investment in the future."

Ian snorted. "Planning for your retirement? Good idea—it might be sooner than you think."

"Not soon enough to do you any good, Mitchell. You've never been anything but a contender, and you never will be. Not with me around."

49

Ian's face turned red, and the cords in his neck stood out. "Maybe you won't be around much longer," he muttered.

Doug leaned across the table and grabbed Ian by the shirt. "Are you threatening me?" he shouted. "Everybody heard you this time. Why don't you go ahead and admit that you already tried to kill me twice today?"

As Joe and Frank moved to separate the two, Ian said, "Because I didn't, that's why. But I can understand why somebody would." He shrugged off Joe's hands and picked up his plate. "Excuse me, everybody. The sight of that guy ruins my appetite."

The table was silent after Ian left. Finally Catherine said, "Can we all please try to enjoy the rest of our meal? The food is getting cold."

After watching Catherine for a moment, Frank scattered a few dots of harissa on the mixture of vegetables and grain and took a bite. It was delicious, but his tongue tingled from the sauce. He glanced over at Joe, who nodded his approval.

"*Aarrggh!*" With a strangled cry, Doug suddenly surged up from his chair. His eyes were bulging, his face was scarlet, and he was clutching his mouth with both hands.

# 6 Hot Stuff

Everyone at the table jumped up. Doug continued to gasp and clutch his mouth.

Joe ran behind him, put his arms around Doug's chest, and placed his clenched fist just under Doug's rib cage. Joe was about to perform the Heimlich maneuver, to clear whatever was caught in Doug's throat, but Doug pushed his hands away.

"No, not choking," he gasped. "Water!"

Frank quickly passed him a glass. Doug drank half of it, panted for a couple of seconds, and drank the other half. Tears streamed down his cheeks, and sweat soaked his forehead.

Frank studied him for a moment, then picked up Doug's plate, sniffed it, and took a taste with his little finger.

"What is it?" Catherine demanded. "What's wrong?"

Frank smiled grimly. "Somebody must have thought Doug likes his spaghetti spicy," he replied. "They poured about half a bowl of that harissa stuff over it."

Everyone looked at the bowl of fiery sauce. It was nearly empty.

"How terrible!" Catherine said. "But who. . . ?"

"Who threatened to kill me two minutes ago?" exclaimed Doug. He mopped his face with his napkin.

"But Ian wouldn't—" Catherine began.

"Why do you always stand up for him?" Doug said angrily. "I know that you two used to be good friends, but you told me that was all over with."

"It is, but I still know what he's like. He wouldn't try to hurt you. Maybe someone made a joke that went wrong."

"Well, I'm not laughing. My tongue's burning!"

Catherine took his hand. "Come with me to the kitchen," she said. "I'll get you an ice cube."

Frank moved around the table and took the empty chair next to Joe. "See anything?" he asked quietly.

Joe wrinkled his nose in disgust. "Not a thing. I was too busy trying to keep Doug and Ian from breaking plates on each other's heads. How about you?"

"Same here. Could Ian have slipped that sauce onto Doug's pasta without you seeing him?"

Joe shook his head. "Maybe. But he would

have had to be really quick about it. Who else?"
He glanced around. "Catherine, Philip, and
Khaled were the only other ones close enough."

"You left someone out," Frank said, smiling.

Joe gave him a puzzled look. "I did? Who?"

"You." Frank grinned and dodged the elbow
aimed at his ribs. Before Joe could take another
shot, Catherine returned to the table.

"Frank, Joe," she said, "you aren't even trying
your couscous. Don't you like our cooking?"

Frank quickly returned to his seat and picked
up his fork, but before he put the forkful of
couscous in his mouth, he took a tiny nibble from
the corner. Across the table, Joe was doing the
same.

Their joker, whoever he was, might have been
acting on a special grudge against Doug. But
while he had the harissa in his hands, he could
have decided to flavor a few other dinners as well.
Why take a chance on scorched tonsils?

After dinner there was still enough light for a
game of volleyball. Frank and Joe ended up on
opposite sides, and so did Ian and Doug. Everyone was playing full tilt, with lots of wicked
spiking, but Doug and Ian were especially vicious. They did their best to slam the ball at each
other's faces and stomachs, even if it meant
sending the ball out of bounds and losing the
point.

Finally the captain of Ian's team, a guy from
Hawaii everyone called Kana, called a halt. "If

53

you and Doug want a grudge match," he said, "put up a hoop and do some one-on-one. We're playing a team game here. You're either on the team or off it."

"Why don't you talk to the big enchilada?" Ian demanded. "He started it."

Kana gave a snort of exasperation. "I don't *care* who started it! It's finished. Got it?"

After that, the two rivals calmed down. Then Ian's team took the game and he gloated so openly that Doug looked ready to chew the net. Frank and Joe took his elbows and hustled him into the villa before he and Ian started again.

Afterward the Hardys went up to their room and flipped to see who got the shower first. Joe won. Frank was jotting down some notes about everything that had happened during the day when someone knocked on the door.

It was Doug.

"I have to talk to you," he said. He sat down on the edge of the bed. "This harassment is getting on my nerves. I ought to be thinking about my strategy for the meet. Instead I keep wondering what direction the next blow is going to come from. You and Joe have to do something."

"We just got here," Frank pointed out.

"I know, I know. I'm not criticizing you or trying to put you on the spot. But unless you can stop it, I'm going to have to do something myself."

"Such as?"

Doug cracked his knuckles. "I don't know," he said. "Tell the press what's been going on, for a start. I can't say who I think is behind the harassment, not without proof. But it ought to be pretty obvious."

"You're talking about Ian?" asked Frank.

"Who else? He—"

There was a banging on the door, and they heard Catherine calling urgently, "Frank! Joe!"

Frank sprang to the door and pulled it open.

Catherine grabbed his hand. "Come, quickly!"

She led him down the hallway. Doug was close behind them. Near the head of the stairs, she stopped. The stairway had been blocked off with chairs, and there was a wet patch on the floor next to the top stair.

"You see?" she said. "It was the smell I noticed first."

Frank sniffed, then knelt down and touched the wet patch. "Wax?" he said.

She nodded. "If I had come upstairs a little later, or if someone else had come along first—"

In his mind Frank saw somebody step on the slippery spot and go headlong down the stairs. "We could have had a very serious accident," he said. "Where do you usually keep the wax?"

"In the broom closet just across the hall."

"Locked?"

"No. I never . . . It didn't seem necessary. My guests here are my friends."

Frank's face was grim. "Someone isn't acting so

friendly," he said. "We'd better clean this up before somebody needs to use the stairs."

With Joe joining in, the four of them managed to strip the wax from the floor in record time. But before going to sleep, Frank and Joe walked through the silent hallways of the villa. They looked around for more booby traps, but everything seemed normal and safe. Apparently the malicious prankster had finished work for the night.

Frank pushed his chair back from the breakfast table and said, "I'll go find Catherine. She can tell us how to get into town and where to cash traveler's checks once we're there."

"Okay," Joe replied. "I'll get our shopping list from upstairs and meet you on the terrace."

The door to Catherine's office was open. Frank started to go in, then hesitated. Catherine was deep in conversation with the bearded middle-aged man Frank had seen chatting with the two roofers the day before. She noticed Frank and motioned him in.

"Emil," she said, "this is Frank Hardy, one of the investigators I told you of. Frank, please meet Emil Molitor, who was my uncle's best friend."

"Yours, too, I hope, my dear," the man said.

He offered his hand to Frank, who remembered the leaflets he had seen in the studio and said, "Molitor, sir? The Molitor Gallery in Paris?"

56

"Yes, indeed," Molitor replied. He looked surprised and a little wary.

"Emil handled all my uncle's sculptures and prints," Catherine explained. "Jacques used to say that he owed everything to Emil."

"Not to me," Molitor said. "To his own talent." He started to go, then turned back to Catherine. "It is agreed, then? I shall bring my things this afternoon. I do not think I shall get in your way, but for your own protection . . ."

Catherine nodded. "Thank you, Emil. I'm beginning to think I need all the help I can get."

After Molitor left, Frank asked Catherine about getting into town and where he could cash traveler's checks.

"But there is no problem with the checks," she said. "I can cash them for you. How much do you need?"

While Frank countersigned the checks, she unlocked her desk drawer, removed a wad of crisp new bills, and counted some out.

"Here you are," she said. "Do you want to take my car? Or if you prefer, you can borrow the motorcycles in the parking area. The keys are always there."

"We'll borrow your car if you don't mind. But another time I'd like to see the area from a bike."

"Will you be back in time for lunch?"

"Oh, sure," Frank replied. "We're just going to do a few errands and take a look at the town."

An hour later, the Hardys were wandering through a maze of steep, narrow cobblestoned streets. The houses on either side were so old that they seemed to lean toward each other. Now and then the boys glimpsed the ruins of a castle atop a hill.

Joe stopped abruptly in front of a shop. "You know," he said, pointing to a beret in the window, "that would look terrific on Iola. Let's find out how much it is."

"Okay," Frank said, rolling his eyes. If Joe brought home a French beret for his girlfriend, Frank would certainly have to get one for *his* girlfriend, Callie, as well.

The storekeeper helped them pick out two berets and Frank handed him the money for them. Suddenly the man's smile faded and his eyes narrowed.

"Wait, please," he said, reaching for the telephone. As he waited to be connected, he held the bill Frank had given him up to the light.

Frank and Joe looked at each other. Something must be wrong with the bill. Frank stared at it. It was bigger than American money, more colorful as well. In the right hand corner was a picture of a castle, and on the left side a man's face. Frank had no idea who the man was, but he looked familiar. Had he seen his features somewhere before, in a book or something? Or maybe he'd just seen that face on another two-hundred-franc note.

After a few tense, silent minutes, two police officers walked in and began talking rapidly to the shopkeeper, who gave them the bill. They in turn held it up to the light, then one of them asked the Hardys where it had come from. Frank told them. They seemed to know Catherine's name. One of them phoned her.

When he got off the telephone, he said, "Please excuse this inconvenience, messieurs. Mademoiselle Dombray confirms what you have told me. Unhappily this note is not genuine, and I must seize it for evidence. I will give you a receipt."

Frank took another bill from his wallet. "What about this one?" he asked. "Is it good? We still want those two berets."

The shopkeeper studied the bill, smiled, and put it in the drawer. As he handed them the package and their change, the police officer finished writing the receipt for the phony bill.

"Do you get a lot of counterfeit money around here?" Joe asked.

The officer looked very uncomfortable. "Forgive me," he said, "but I am not able to say anything about that."

"Meaning, yes," Joe told Frank as soon as they were on the street again.

Frank frowned. "Um. Let's go back to the villa and see if Catherine can tell us anything."

As soon as she saw them, Catherine started apologizing for their encounter with the police.

She seemed sure that the phony bill had come from her that morning.

"There was very much counterfeit money in this region a year or two ago," she explained. "Then it mysteriously stopped appearing."

"Were the crooks ever found?" asked Frank.

"I do not know. It is a very bad sign that this should start again, and at my inn. Do you suppose that this, too, is part of the jinx that everyone is talking about?"

"Don't worry," Joe said. "If it is, we'll put a stop to it—along with all the other dirty tricks."

Catherine shook her head. "If only you are right. I will not be able to take much more of this. You Hardys are my last hope."

After lunch Doug took Frank and Joe over to Almanarre Beach—he wanted to try out a new sail. They helped him mount the mast and rig the wishbone, the double shaft that he gripped to hold the mast upright. Then they sat down on the sand to watch him. A lot of other people were on the beach watching, too.

Doug sailed each point of the wind in turn, then began slaloming, jumping the incoming waves in a burst of spray. Just down the beach from the Hardys, a guy in khaki shorts fitted a huge telephoto lens on his camera and started clicking off shots of Doug. No question, Doug was a star. He even had a small plane circling over him, probably with another photographer aboard.

Doug tacked far upwind, then started a speed run on a broad reach parallel to the beach. His form was perfect. His straight arms, legs, and back were like three sides of a square, with the taut sail closing the box.

The photographer next to the Hardys was taking pictures as fast as his motor drive would let him. Out over the water, the single-engine plane circled lower, then lower still.

"Look out!" Joe yelled.

Doug was making at least thirty knots when the plane swooped down just in front of him. As he instinctively ducked, the prop wash from the plane battered his sail from one side, then the other.

The sail shivered, then suddenly flipped onto the opposite tack. Doug let out a shout and released the wishbone. A moment later he was doing a high-speed somersault into the water.

# 7 Trouble in the Air

The Hardys sprang to their feet and raced down to the edge of the water.

"Where's Doug?" Joe demanded. "Can you see him? Is he all right?"

Together they stared out toward the spot where their friend had just taken a hard spill.

"Not yet," Frank replied. He shaded his eyes with his hand. "Maybe we'd better . . . No, there he is! He's swimming over to his board to bring it in."

"He looks pretty shaky," Joe said.

Frank nodded. "You would, too, in his place. Hitting the water at that speed is like hitting a concrete wall. Come on, let's go out and give him a hand."

The boys swam out and helped Doug bring the board back to the beach.

Doug sprawled full-length on the sand. "I'm

going to take a few minutes off," he said. "That guy really shook me up this time."

"This time?" Joe repeated. "You mean he's done it before?"

Doug frowned. "Either him or somebody else, yeah. It was a couple of days ago, before you guys got here. At the time I figured it was just a mistake."

"It's not the kind of mistake you make twice," Joe said.

"No, it looked pretty deliberate to me," Frank agreed. "Deliberate, and dangerous. Do you have any idea where the plane could have come from?"

"No . . . Wait, there's a charter service at the airport. It might have been from there."

Frank exchanged a look with Joe. "I think we'd better go over and have a talk with the manager," he told Doug. "He's bound to keep records of his customers. This may be our first real break in the case."

"Think so?" Doug rubbed his chin. "I don't know, it could have been an accident both times. Maybe somebody wanted a closer look at my rig and didn't pay attention to where they were flying. I wouldn't make a big deal about it."

"Maybe you're right, Doug," said Joe. "But we have to check out every lead, right? Otherwise we might be letting an important piece of evidence slip past us."

"Yeah, I guess so. I just don't want to see you wasting your time. Still . . . You want to take my car? I'm going to rest a little longer, then maybe try another run."

"You want us to come back here for you?"

Doug shook his head. "Naw, I can sail across the bay and land at the little beach near the villa. I calm down faster on a board than anywhere."

"Okay, thanks," Frank said, taking the car keys. "See you later."

The charter service occupied a small white hangar on the far side of the airport. The sign over the door advertised rentals, charters, and flying lessons. The sign *on* the door said that the office was closed for ten minutes. It didn't say when the ten minutes had started.

Joe and Frank strolled out onto the concrete parking area to admire the aircraft. They ranged all the way from small single-engine training planes to a luxurious ten-passenger executive jet. At the far end were three helicopters of varying sizes. There was even a flimsy-looking ultralight with its single seat right out in the open.

Frank nudged his brother. "The third one down," he said. "Doesn't that look like the plane that buzzed Doug?"

"It sure does," Joe replied. "Let's see if the engine is still warm."

As they were walking over to the small airplane, a car pulled up next to the office and a man in light blue coveralls climbed out.

"Hello," he called. "You need something?"

The Hardys went over and introduced themselves.

"We'd like some information, if you don't mind," Frank said. He explained what had happened at Almanarre Beach half an hour before.

"That plane over there looks like the one we saw," he concluded. "Can you tell me if it's been up today?"

"I don't know if I ought to be talking about my customers," the man said. "Still, if somebody has been doing dangerous stunts . . . Yes, I rented it this afternoon. It just came back in about twenty minutes ago. I left to get a cup of coffee right afterward."

"What can you tell us about the person who rented it?"

The man hesitated again. "His name's Highgate, Tom Highgate. He told me he's a sports photographer."

"Has he rented from you before?"

"No, this was the first time."

"Are you sure?"

"Uh-huh. Unless he took up a plane one day when I was off on a flight and my partner was running the office."

"Was he alone?" Joe asked.

"Yes. I don't know how he was planning to fly

the plane and take pictures at the same time. For a little more money I would have piloted him myself."

"Maybe for what he was planning to do, he needed to be alone," said Frank. "Did he show you any identification?"

"Of course," the man said. "All his papers were in order. But . . . Listen, I really can't tell you anything else. A charter pilot has to know how to keep his mouth shut. We fly a lot of important people—movie stars, corporate executives, government officials. If it got around that we were spreading gossip about a customer, we'd be out of business."

Joe started to argue with him, but Frank cut in. "We understand," he said. "But will you do this for us? I'll leave you our telephone number. If this Highgate guy shows up again to rent a plane, will you let us know? I guarantee it won't get back to him."

"Well . . . no harm in that, I guess. Sure, I'll do that. Say, you guys wouldn't like a bird's-eye view of the area, would you? I've got some empty places in my schedule that I'd like to fill up."

"Sorry," said Frank. "Maybe another time."

They drove back to the villa and found that the iron gate at the head of the driveway was closed. When Frank went to unlatch it, a burly man in jeans and a plaid shirt got out of a parked car and came toward him.

66

Frank clenched his fists and glanced around. How many of them were there? He didn't see anyone else. Was this really the ambush it looked like? He sensed Joe at his side, ready for anything.

The burly man stopped a few feet away. "You're the Hardys, right?" he said. "The detectives?"

"Who are you?" Frank demanded.

"Jack Cortese, *Wind and Wave* magazine," he replied. "Are you here to stop the harassment campaign against Doug Newman? Is it true that he's losing his nerve?"

"No comment," said Joe.

"I hear he took quite a spill this afternoon. One of our free-lancers says he got a terrific picture of it, maybe even cover material. I can see the headline now: Champ Bites Wave. Or maybe it ought to say Newman Takes a Dive? What do you think?"

The reporter was obviously trying to goad them into talking to him. Frank silently shook his head and swung the gate open.

"We've got a pool going in the pressroom," Cortese continued. "Newman versus the jinx. Some of the guys think he'll get hurt too badly to be in the meet. Some of the others are betting that even if he gets that far, he'll be too off his form to win the Cup a third time. Any comments?"

"Just one," Frank said, getting behind the wheel again. "You're standing in the way of our car."

He revved the engine and started forward.

The reporter jumped aside. "Just wait, smart aleck," he shouted. "You'll talk to me sooner or later!"

"Later, I hope," Frank said as Joe got back in the car after closing the gate. They rolled down the driveway and parked behind the villa.

"Right," Joe replied. "Why do I get the feeling that everybody knows more about this case than we do? And since when did *Wind and Wave* start following our careers as detectives?"

"Since we got involved with Doug and the upcoming meet," said Frank. "And that's a very interesting fact right there, isn't it?"

Doug was in the living room, talking to Catherine and to Molitor, the art dealer. As the Hardys approached, he was saying, "I'm sorry, Emil. I'd like to help you, but the Cup isn't mine. Not yet, anyway."

"It would be only for a day or two, just to photograph the engravings. For my next show of Dombray's work, I plan to have enormous enlargements of the Almanarre Cup on the rear wall of the gallery. It is almost unknown, except to those in the world of sailboarding."

Doug shook his head. "It's not up to me. I told you, the local museum has custody of it. Why not take your pictures there?"

Molitor sniffed. "It is not a few snapshots that I need," he said. "This is delicate work. It requires an experienced photographer with a properly equipped studio."

He turned to Catherine. "My dear, perhaps you, as your uncle's heir, could convince the museum authorities to release the Cup to me."

Catherine looked troubled. "I don't think so, Emil," she said. "I wouldn't want anything to happen to it just before the meet. Maybe afterward? If Doug wins, you can ask him to lend it to you, and if he doesn't win, I promise to speak to the people at the museum."

Molitor looked as if he wanted to go on arguing, but Catherine said, "Will you excuse me, Emil? I have to make sure everything is going well for dinner."

"And I need to wash some of the salt off my hide," Doug said with a smile. "See you later."

Molitor watched them go. His face was angry, but when he turned and saw Frank and Joe, he smiled and wished them a good evening.

Doug finished dessert, a sponge cake with whipped cream and fresh raspberries, and sighed. "That was terrific, Catherine," he said, "but now I'm going to have to work off all those calories."

He turned to the Hardys. "What do you say, guys? Want to take your boards out? The wind's holding steady, and we've got another hour or two of daylight left."

"Great," said Joe and Frank, almost in unison.

"You'd better watch yourselves," Ian said from farther down the table. "Things have a way of happening around Dougie-boy. Mostly bad things."

Doug pushed himself back from the table, hard enough to make the dishes rattle. "Are you threatening me, Ian?" he demanded.

"Me?" his rival replied in a mocking tone. "I'd never do a thing like that to a champion like you. Or even to an about-to-be-ex-champion."

Doug's face reddened. "Just wait until Saturday," he said. "I'll just plain blow your doors off."

"Oh, for sure," Ian said. "For sure. If you manage to stay on your board, that is."

Frank sensed that this scene wasn't going to do anybody any good. "Come on, Doug," he said, taking his arm. "Joe and I have been here two days already and we haven't even gotten our boards wet."

For a moment Doug tried to pull his arm away. Then he nodded, gave Ian one final stare, and followed the Hardys upstairs to change back into swimsuits.

The wind and surf were just right for wave jumping. Frank and Joe went easy, making little jumps and laughing out loud each time they landed and took a bucket of spray in the face.

70

For a while Doug stayed next to them, but he didn't seem comfortable taking it easy. He only knew one way to windsurf: flat out. Soon he was cutting back and forth, working up the speed to leap higher and higher. The Hardys stopped their own jumping to watch a champion at work.

The wind was stronger now, and the waves were getting higher. Doug tacked to starboard, then aimed his board directly at an incoming roller. As the front of the board came up, he seemed to lift the board with his feet. Suddenly he was upside down in midair. The bottom of his board was reaching for the sky, and the tip of his mast was aimed at the wave. A forward roll, one of the toughest maneuvers in boardsailing!

Frank was drawing a breath to shout congratulations when Doug's mast seemed to come loose at the base. The loss of support threw Doug completely off balance. He twisted his upper body sideways, trying to get out from under the falling board.

A second wave caught the tip of Doug's sail. The mast seesawed around wildly. Suddenly it cracked Doug across the forehead. Stunned, he let go of the wishbone. The mast and sail flapped sideways, and the board landed upside down in the surging water.

Joe stared, horror-struck. "His feet," he shouted to Frank. "They're caught in the foot straps! He's sure to drown!"

# 8 A Deadly Sport

Joe angled his board toward the spot where Doug had disappeared under the water. It was only a few yards, but they seemed endless. He took his left hand off the wishbone and slapped the quick-release buckle of his harness. For a moment it seemed to stick, but then the straps parted. He shrugged them off his shoulders and grabbed the wishbone again.

Up ahead, Doug's board, still upside-down, was drifting toward the beach. The split fin sticking up from the water made the board look like a shark. For Doug that board might turn out to be as deadly as any shark could ever be.

Joe sensed that Frank was just behind him, but he had no time to check. As his board came level with Doug's, he let the sail go and made a running dive into the water.

Doug was farther back on his board than Joe had remembered. By the time Joe located Doug's feet and started to disentangle them from the foot straps, Joe's lungs felt as if they were bursting. He surfaced, gulped a breath, then dove under again.

One foot loose. He was removing the other from the foot strap when he felt the freed foot start to slip from his hand. What if he released Doug from his board, only to see him sink to the bottom?

Joe came up for air a second time and felt a hand on his shoulder.

Frank leaned his head close and shouted, "I'll take his shoulders and try to bring him up. You get that foot free!"

Joe nodded and grabbed a deep breath. As he started under, a wave caught Doug's upside-down board and cracked the edge of it against Joe's wrist. It hurt a lot, but he had no attention to spare for that now.

He located the trapped foot once more and worked at freeing it from the padded cloth strap. Tugging at the strap, he twisted the heel one way, then another. Just when he was starting to think that he could never succeed in time, the foot slipped out. Doug was free!

Free, yes, but in time?

Joe swam to the board and gripped the edge, panting. Across from him, Frank was holding Doug's head and chest above water. Doug's eyes were shut and he had an ugly welt across his forehead.

Frank leaned his head close to Doug's face and listened intently. After a moment he looked up and said, "He's breathing. If I take him in on his board, can you manage the other two?"

Joe nodded and looked around. The boards he and Frank had been sailing were still only a few yards away. He helped Frank hoist Doug onto the damaged board and swam across to start collecting the others.

By the time Joe reached the beach, it was nearly dark. Doug was sitting on the sand, holding his head. He looked up, met Joe's eyes, and said, "Thanks, guy. I owe you a great big one."

"Hey, that's okay," Joe replied, reddening. "How are you feeling?"

"Like I just spent a week in a washing machine. I've had some close calls now and then, but this one . . ." He shuddered and took a deep breath.

Frank returned with their towels. Doug took one and pulled it tightly around his shoulders. After a long silence, he said, "What I want to know is why—" He pushed himself to his feet and walked over to his beached sailboard. He knelt in the sand and studied the mast mount for a moment. When he stood up again, his face was red with anger.

"That didn't break by itself," he said. "Somebody tampered with it! And I know who!"

He started up the steep path to the villa, the broken mount in his hand. Frank and Joe were right behind him.

"For somebody who just missed drowning," Frank said in a low voice, "he's got a lot of energy all of a sudden."

Joe glanced sharply at his brother. "He *was* drowning," he said. "No mistake about that."

"I know. But was he supposed to? Or was it a stunt that went wrong?"

Joe knitted his brow. "A stunt? Whose stunt? Not Doug's—you saw his face after he discovered the broken mast mount."

"Uh-huh. Interesting, wasn't it? It looked to me like he was indignant. Why indignant? That's what I'd like to know. Come on, I have a hunch the Villa Dombray is going to need a peacekeeping force tonight."

They reached the living room in time to see Doug thrust the broken mount under Ian's nose and hear him say, "Do you know what this is, Mitchell?"

"Sure, Dougie," Ian replied coolly. "It's a broken mast mount. As a matter of fact, it looks kind of familiar. Is that the one you practiced on before you did a job on mine?"

"It's *my* mast mount," Doug said, "and it snapped on me in the middle of a forward roll."

"Yeah? Well, that's as good an excuse as any, I guess. Are you sure a sea gull didn't fly past your face and frighten you?"

A couple of listeners laughed at Ian's crack. Obviously they had all heard about Doug's encounter with the airplane.

Doug reddened. "No joke, Ian. I know you messed with this mount, and I'm not going to let you get away with it. What's the matter? Is it starting to dawn on you that I'm going to beat you again this time? You figure if you cripple me, maybe you can win the Cup at last? No way, Charlie!"

Catherine hurried into the room and put her hand on Doug's arm, but he brushed her aside and continued. "I'm going to win the Cup this year if I have to do it with one leg in a cast, and no bag of dirty tricks is going to stop me."

"I won't need any dirty tricks to stop you," said Ian. His voice was so taut with anger that it sounded as if it might snap. "I'm going to outsail and outpoint you, Dougie-boy. And afterward I'm going to pound you into the sand headfirst like a tent stake."

"Ian," Catherine pleaded. "Ian, please!"

"Everybody here knows whose board was tampered with first," Ian went on. "Don't think you can cover your tracks with a little accident of your own."

Frank stepped forward. This had gone far enough. "It wasn't such a little accident," he said quietly. "Take a look at Doug's forehead. That falling mast put him out for the count. If we hadn't been right there, he would have drowned."

Ian looked at Doug's face and his expression changed. "Hey, listen," he began, "I didn't . . ."

Frank took the broken mount from Doug and handed it to Ian. "Is this the same kind of damage that was done to yours?" he asked.

Ian studied it. "Well, it's a different model, of course, but yeah, basically."

"How long would it take somebody to tamper with a mount that way?"

Ian frowned. "I don't know, not long I guess. Not if they knew exactly what they were doing. What would you say, Doug, a couple of minutes?"

"Why are you asking *me?*" Doug demanded.

"Oh, come off it," Ian replied, rolling his eyes. "I'm asking you because you know more about sailboards than practically anyone around."

"Oh," Doug said. He seemed startled by the unexpected compliment. "Well, yeah, it looks like someone put a lot of strain on the joint from the side. You could probably do it with a big screwdriver. The joint's not built to take pressure from that direction—it doesn't have to be."

He smiled. "Hey, Ian, remember that beach party at Hookipa a few years back, when Jim Slater couldn't find a bottle opener and used his mast mount instead? And the next morning he was shooting the tube when it went wonky on him? What a wipeout!"

"Sure," Ian replied, grinning. "And he spent the rest of the meet trying to scrounge a ride from the rest of us. But nobody brought spare boards in those days."

"Brought? Nobody *had* spare boards! The

game's changed a lot, hasn't it? Hey, I'm sorry I blew up before, but I was so sure . . . "

Ian looked at him warily. "Forget it. You had a right to be mad. I'm mad, too, and once we find whoever's in back of this, he's in for some big trouble."

Catherine took advantage of the change in mood. "How about some fruit and cheese?" she suggested. "I'll bring it to the dining room."

The two rivals walked off together, followed by a clump of other competitors. Frank and Joe looked at each other, and Joe started to laugh.

"Good work, Frank," he said. "Everyone's buddies again."

Frank nodded. "Great. But somebody fiddled with that mount, and if we don't find out who pretty soon, they're going to be at it again. And next time it might not be so easy to keep them from killing each other!"

By midnight the villa was dark and quiet. Joe took a last look out the window before going to bed. It was a still night, and the sky was clear. The moon, just rising, cast a jagged yellow path across the waters of the bay. He couldn't imagine a more peaceful scene. By listening hard, he could even hear the louder shushing sound of the waves on the beach at Almanarre.

Suddenly he stiffened. Between the crash of waves he could hear a set of footsteps moving stealthily along the gravel path right below him.

He leaned out and peered into the shadows. At first he couldn't see anything, then he made out a dark form that flitted across a patch of moonlight and vanished in the direction of the equipment shed. A moment later he was sure he heard the shed door open.

Frank was already half-asleep, but he sat up instantly when Joe touched his shoulder. "Quick," Joe whispered. "Someone's in the shed."

They pulled on jams and crept down the stairs. At the door, Frank said, "We'll split up, circle the house in different directions, and meet in front of the shed."

Joe nodded and started to the left, walking carefully on the grass. He didn't want to make any noise that might scare off the intruder. As he picked his way around the chairs scattered about the lawn, he was grateful that the moon was high enough and bright enough to help him see his way.

He turned the corner of the house. Directly ahead, the black shape of the equipment shed loomed against the sky. He thought he saw a dim light flicker in the window, but it was gone before he could be sure.

Where was Frank? Joe stood very still and peered into the shadows. Suddenly he heard a faint noise and saw a darker rectangle in the dark front wall of the shed. The door was opening!

He held his breath. Was that a movement in the

shadows? Just as he was taking a cautious step forward, there was a loud clatter and a suppressed cry from the far side of the house.

Instantly he heard running footsteps and saw a dark form dart across the moonlit terrace. As Joe sprang into motion, the pale oval of a face glanced back at him. The intruder seemed to hesitate for a moment, then swerved to run toward the path that wound down the side of the cliff to the beach.

Was there a boat waiting below? Joe put on a new burst of speed. The moon was just bright enough to show him the white posts of the guardrails on either side. He ran headlong, letting the steep slope carry him until he felt as if he were barely touching the ground.

The fleeing form was just a few yards ahead now, almost within reach. Boat or no boat, he couldn't possibly get away. Joe was nerving himself to make a flying tackle when the shadowy form veered to the right and vanished into a patch of darkness.

Clenching his teeth, Joe sprinted still faster and followed the form around the curve in the path. He had just enough time to notice the gap in the guardrail, then the ground disappeared from under his feet.

He twisted his body desperately, with a skill gained from years of practicing jump shots, and grabbed for the edge of the path. His hands slipped in the dust, then touched a spiny bush growing from the side of the cliff. He gripped it with every bit of strength he had and held on as the momentum of his fall slammed him into the cliff. For one instant he looked down at the rocky beach, thirty feet below.

"Frank," he called, fighting for breath. *"Frank!"*

"I'm coming," his brother called from somewhere up above. "Where are you?"

"Down here—the cliff path!" He found a tiny toehold in the cliff and started trying to pull himself up to the path. Suddenly he froze. The bush he was clinging to, the only thing between him and a terrible fall, was starting to pull loose from the thin soil.

*"Frank,"* he called again, more urgently. "Frank, *hurry!*"

# 9 The Hanging Bush

Joe gripped the bush tightly and cautiously brushed his feet across the face of the cliff. If he could find any toehold at all, he could take some of the weight off his hands. But even such a slight motion caused the bush to slip another heart-stopping half inch. How much longer could its slender roots hold in the thin, stony soil? How much more strain could they take?

"Frank!" he called again.

"I'm here," his brother called back from nearby. "Where are you? What's wrong?"

"Down here—on the cliff, below the path! Grab me! Quick, this bush is pulling loose!"

Propelled by the urgency in his brother's voice, Frank ran down the treacherous path. He saw the gap in the guardrail, skidded to a stop, and flung himself on his stomach. Now his head and shoulders were over the edge. Where was Joe?

He gasped. His younger brother was almost a yard down from the path, clinging to a gnarled bush that didn't look as if it could support a good-sized squirrel. Frank reached down for him, but the gap between them was too big. Joe was staring up at him with the beginning of real fear in his eyes. Down below, a long way down, the jagged rocks waited like rows of shark teeth.

"Hang on," Frank shouted. "You're okay, just hang on!"

"I'll hang on," Joe replied. "It's the bush that worries me."

Frank wriggled back from the edge and looked around. The path offered nothing for him to cling to, and if he tried to climb down the cliff, they might both plummet to the shore. What could he use for a rope? His shirt? Too flimsy. If only he had put on jeans instead of jams!

The gap in the guardrail was about four feet wide. Was the rail still around somewhere? He searched the shadows. No luck. In the eerie moonlight, the white post by the edge of the cliff looked like the ghostly finger of a buried giant, beckoning to him. . . .

Of course! He scrambled around, stretched his legs on either side of the sturdy post, and locked his ankles together. Then he leaned far out over the edge and reached down. His fingers almost brushed Joe's arm. Close, so close, but not quite close enough.

"Joe," he called. "Can you let go with your left hand and grab my wrist? Left hand!"

"I'll . . . try," Joe panted. "But the bush . . ."

Frank stretched down as far as he could and held his breath. Joe's hand released its grip on the fragile bush and groped blindly across the face of the cliff. Just as his fingers found Frank's wrist and closed on it, the roots of the bush finally gave way.

Joe let out a cry and swung sideways, supported only by his grasp on his brother's wrist.

"Hold on," Frank shouted once again. He inched forward, ignoring the rocks that scraped his stomach and thighs, and stretched out his other arm. Could he . . . ?

Suddenly he felt Joe's wrist under his fingertips and closed his hand like a vise. "I've got you," he called. "But I don't think I can lift you. Can you manage to climb?"

"I don't know, I'll try."

The strain on Frank's arms grew heavier. Then Joe's other hand was grasping his arm, too. He put everything he had left into a strong, steady pull.

"On three," he called. "One . . . two . . . *three!*"

Joe's feet scrambled at the side of the cliff and he surged upward, clearing the edge and falling heavily across Frank's back.

"Oof!" said Frank. "Next time, watch where you land!"

"I'll do that," Joe replied, fighting to catch his breath. "Thanks, buddy."

"Don't mention it. But don't make it a habit."

"I won't," Joe promised, panting. "I'll bet I have a gray streak in my hair after that."

"Always keep up with the fashions. I think someone's coming."

The Hardys struggled to their feet just as Emil came down the path, a flashlight in his hand. The bright beam swung out toward the water, then settled on the two brothers.

"Are you all right?" he demanded. "I heard a call for help. I was afraid that the bad luck of this place was claiming another victim."

"We're okay, thanks," Frank said. "But it wasn't bad luck that pried that guardrail loose. Somebody wanted to create an accident."

Joe grabbed Frank's arm. "Hey, listen!"

Just off the beach, a powerful outboard motor roared into life. A moment later the sound was fading into the darkness.

"Any bets that that was our somebody?" asked Joe.

"Not from me," Frank said grimly.

"But you are hurt, both of you," Emil exclaimed. "You must come back to the villa at once to have your wounds tended!"

"They're not wounds," Frank said. "Just a few scrapes." But as he said it he realized that he was aching all over. And if he felt like that, Joe must feel a lot worse. He had been through a lot more, after all.

"I guess I could use a shower and a few Band-Aids," he admitted. "The rocks around here are pretty jagged. Come on, Joe, let's climb the cliff. But this time we'll stay on the path!"

They were walking up the steps to the terrace when Frank noticed a faint, flickering light in the window of the equipment shed. "Joe," he said quietly. "Someone's in there."

They crept up to the door, which was a few inches ajar, and peeked in. In the far corner, near the racks of sails, was a pile of cardboard cartons. Flames were starting to lick at the lowest cartons. Another minute, and the whole shed might be afire. And right in front of the spreading fire was the silhouette of someone who seemed to be fanning the flames!

Joe turned toward the villa and shouted, "Fire!" Then he followed Frank into the shed, which was filling up with lung-searing smoke.

"Help me," a voice called. "I've nearly got it under control."

It was Philip Barstow, the sailboard designer. He had a rolled-up blanket in his hands and he was beating at the flames with it. But hadn't he been waving it at the fire only a moment before? As he kicked and stomped the smoldering cartons, Joe decided that question could wait until the fire was out.

Others, alerted by Joe's cry, had come out to

help, though the fumes were making his eyes tear too much to see who they were. For a few moments he was afraid that the fire might get the better of them.

Then Catherine's voice said, "Stand aside, let me through!" An instant later came the loud hiss of a foam fire extinguisher. The smoke in the shed grew even thicker and more choking. Joe followed the others out the door, leaned against the wall of the shed, and drew in big gulps of the fresh night air.

Fresh night air, but with a strange smell that reminded him of boyhood camping trips. Kerosene! Someone standing near him had kerosene on his hands or clothes. But why? The only use he could think of for kerosene was to start a fire. . . . And somebody had just tried to do exactly that!

He glanced around. Philip, Emil, and Olaf were on one side of him, and Doug and Catherine on the other. Frank was still at the door, peering into the shed. And who was that in the shadow of the hedge, a few feet away? It looked like Ian, but before Joe could be sure, the figure slipped away. The smell of kerosene could have come from any of them, or even from the interior of the shed.

"Joe," said Frank quietly, "could anyone have gone up the cliff path past us without our knowing?"

"Not a chance," Joe replied.

"That's what I think, too. When I heard you call for help before, I was right here, checking out the equipment shed. And there was no fire in that corner or anywhere else. You see what that means?"

Joe nodded. "It means the guy I was chasing didn't set the fire. Somebody else did."

"It means more than that," Frank continued. "Because when I left here to see what had happened to you, I pulled the door shut and I heard the lock click. Whoever started the fire had to have a key."

Joe glanced around. "Like any of these people here," he said. "By the way, do you smell kerosene?"

Frank sniffed, then shook his head. "All I can smell is smoke," he said. "Why, do you?"

"Not anymore. I thought I did." He straightened up and said, "Philip? How did you happen to spot the fire?"

"I've been expecting something like this," the designer said. "And when I heard somebody shouting out here, I came down to see if my boards were safe. The door of the shed was open and I saw the flames in the corner. Then you guys showed up."

"You didn't call for help?" said Frank.

"I didn't think I needed it. Why wake up the whole neighborhood for nothing?"

"Nothing?" Olaf repeated. "I don't call it nothing if all our gear is burned up! What if all of us at the villa have to drop out just before one of the most important meets of the year? Is that nothing!"

"All I meant—" Philip began.

"He meant he thought he could put it out by himself," Catherine explained. "Perhaps you were right, Philip, but you should have called for help, anyway. The risk was not yours to take."

She looked around. "Come on, everybody," she added, "let's go back to bed. You do not want to spend the day before the meet catching up on your sleep!"

Joe and Frank followed her up the steps to the terrace. At the door, she stopped short and said, "What is this?"

Joe looked over her shoulder, and felt a chilly sensation in his spine. Pinned to the door was a sheet of paper. The pasted-on words had been cut from a magazine, and the message read:

Newman will not come back alive if he goes on the water tomorrow.

# 10 Last Chance

Joe stood by the table in their room, staring down at the threatening note.

"Something about it looks familiar." He rummaged through the pile of stuff in the corner and returned with a magazine. As he flipped through the pages, Frank joined him at the table.

"I thought so," Joe said. "Look at the type in the headline of this article about Doug. The word *Newman* looks just the same as in the note. I'll bet it wouldn't be hard to find the rest in here, too."

Frank nodded. "So whoever made that message cut the words from the latest issue of *Wind and Wave*. The problem is, there was a stack of free copies in the living room yesterday. I guess practically everybody picked one up."

"So that's no help at all," said Joe. "But what about this? Who pinned up the note, and when? First we were all in the shed, fighting the fire, then we were all standing together outside the shed. And when we went back up to the terrace, there was the note. So whoever put it up must have been the last to leave the villa."

"Or someone who went inside before us," Frank added. "Either way, it looks like Barstow is out. He was already in the shed when we arrived, and he was behind us when we found the note."

"Catherine must have been the last out," Joe said. "But she was bringing the fire extinguisher. Could she have stopped and pinned up the note?"

"She could have, sure, but I don't see that happening. Let's face it, with all the confusion, we can't be sure who did what or when. And if you're right about seeing Ian hanging around in the bushes, *he* could have done it. It didn't even have to be someone who came outside. Our baddie could have simply reached out through the open doorway and pinned up the note without ever leaving the villa."

Joe let out a frustrated growl. "So the note is no help at all," he said.

"Maybe not," Frank said slowly. "But why not come at it from the other end? As far as we know, this is the first time in this whole case that a real threat has been made. And it's pretty specific, too. Who? Doug. When? Tomorrow. And where? On the water. That gives me an idea."

The Hardys stayed up a long time discussing Frank's idea and how to put it into action.

After breakfast the next morning, Catherine

asked the Hardys to meet her and Doug in her office. "I'm tired," she began, once they were all sitting down. "Tired and scared. Last night it was the equipment shed. It was only good luck that it was not destroyed, with everything inside it. Tonight we could wake up and find the whole villa in flames."

The telephone on her desk rang. She answered it. "No," she said, "I have no comment. No."

She covered the mouthpiece and looked at Doug. "Someone from *Wind and Wave* wants to know about the fire last night and the threats against you. Do you wish to speak with him?"

Doug grabbed the receiver and said, "This is Doug Newman. Here's a statement for you—I'm going after the Almanarre Cup tomorrow and I intend to win it, threats or no threats. Did you get that? Good, because that's all I have to say."

He slammed the receiver down on the hook and said, "What a bunch of jerks! You know what they say. If you can sail, you sail. If you can't, you write about it."

For a moment he was silent. Then he said, "Getting back to what's been happening here, do you have any idea what they want? It makes no sense!"

"That note we found last night was pretty clear," Frank pointed out. "Whoever 'they' may be, they want you out of the meet."

"You heard what I told that reporter," Doug replied. "I wasn't grandstanding. Threats don't impress me. I'm in the meet to stay—and to win."

"Sure," said Joe. "But what Frank meant is that it looks like you're the real target of this campaign. If that's so, it's not too hard to guess who's behind it."

"You mean Ian," Doug said.

"No," Catherine burst out. "I can't believe it. He's not that . . . that cold-blooded."

"There's nothing cold-blooded about the way he and Doug have been going at each other," said Frank.

He looked over at Doug. "What I don't understand is why you guys dislike each other so much. Ian seems pretty nice when he's not on your case. Why can't you get along?"

Doug started to say something, but Frank cut him off. "I know," he said, "you've been competing against each other for years, and he can't stand always coming out number two. But why does he act like he hates you? What's in back of it?"

Doug shook his head. "I don't really know. We used to get along. Oh, we'd razz each other a lot, the way guys do, but we never gave each other any real grief. Then about a year ago things turned nasty. He started taking cheap shots at me every chance he got. And I . . . well, I'm not the kind of guy who turns his back on something like that. I took a few shots of my own. And before I knew it, we were enemies. I wish I knew why."

Frank met Catherine's eyes and looked at her steadily. Color started rising in her cheeks. "*I* can tell you why," she said suddenly.

"You?" said Doug.

"I'm afraid so. I hoped I wouldn't have to talk about it, but I can't put it off any longer." She turned her chair and looked away from them, toward the window.

"Doug, you know that Ian and I went together for a long time," she continued. "What you don't know is that it was more serious than I ever told you. We even talked of marriage. But then my uncle became ill, and I felt I had to stay here and help take care of him. Ian couldn't understand that. He wanted me to run away with him. And when I refused, he started accusing me of being interested in somebody else."

"Were you?" Doug demanded.

She sighed. "No. I had no energy for such things. But accusing people of doing something often ends by leading them to do just that. It was only after I broke up with Ian that I started looking at you in a new way. He would never believe that. And when I told him that you and I were engaged, he was very, very angry."

"And that's when he started planning to sabotage me," Doug said. He jumped up from his chair. "Where is he? I'm going to pulverize him!"

Catherine sprang up, too, and took Doug's arm. "Wait," she insisted, "you don't understand. Ian is still angry, yes, with you and with me as well.

He continues to say things that hurt me very much. But he would never damage someone else's sailboard or set a building on fire. I *know* him, and I know he could not do such things."

The telephone rang again. She picked it up and listened for a moment, then handed it to Frank.

"Yes?" he said. "I see. When? Okay, thanks very much for letting me know. I'll talk to you later." As he hung up, he caught Joe's eye and gave a slight nod.

"Well, if Ian isn't in back of all this business," Doug was saying, "I wish I knew who was. I've got an important meet tomorrow, and I haven't even been able to *think* about it. I'd do just about anything to help clear up the mystery."

"Really?" Frank said quickly. "I was hoping you felt like that. Joe and I have come up with a plan, but we need your help to pull it off. . . ."

Frank waded out from the beach until the water was above his waist. Then he bent over and struggled into the wet suit he had been carrying under his arm. Fortunately, the wet suit was a little big for him. As far as he could tell, no one had paid the least attention to him. Why should they? Windsurfers and wet suits were as common at Almanarre Beach as bottles of suntan lotion.

Once in the suit, Frank swam farther out, until he was about a hundred yards from the beach. He began treading water. The bay was full of sailboards. He kept a careful eye out for those that might come too close to him. It wasn't easy to sail a board and notice a swimmer's head at the same time.

A sleek-looking board carved a path toward him. He recognized the distinctive red-and-blue sail at once, and the matching wet suit—just like the photo in the magazine. Frank raised his hand and waved, and the rider nodded in reply.

The nod apparently disturbed his balance, because a moment later he lost it and took a spill, only a few feet from Frank. Frank quickly swam over, grabbed the board, and turned it across the wind with the sail on the tail, ready for a fast water-start.

As Frank pushed the boom up and felt the wind begin to lift him onto the board, Doug said, "Remember, guy, my reputation is in your hands!"

Then Frank was up and beginning to plane, while Doug stayed behind, neck-deep in the water. No one had noticed the fast exchange. Anyone who saw the sail and the matching wet suit would believe they were watching Doug Newman at practice for the next day. Even if they noticed that he wasn't sailing as well as usual, they would simply assume that he was off his form. By now practically everyone in the windsurfing world knew about the harassment Doug had been suffering.

It was a great day to be on a board. The strong steady wind called the mistral had started to blow early that morning, and Frank took advantage of it to practice sailing to different points of the wind. The only thing he had to worry about was ending up too far downwind.

Not *quite* the only thing he had to worry about. After all, his role today was a lot like that of a goat staked out to attract the attention of any passing tiger. Unlike the goat, he had chosen the role, but that didn't make it more comfortable.

He glanced eastward, into the sun. Some sort of small craft was in that part of the sky, but he couldn't be sure if it was a plane or a chopper. He would probably find out soon enough.

For now his job was to imitate a champion boardsailor, and he might as well enjoy himself. A fast boom-to-boom jibe brought him onto a broad reach and he really started to steam, hanging in the foot straps and raking the sail all the way back for maximum oomph.

As a whitecap slapped him in the side, he leaned back in the harness, opened his mouth wide, and let out a yell of pure glee.

"That's him," Joe said into the intercom. He pointed toward the red-and-blue sail. The chopper pilot nodded. "Let's keep this distance," Joe continued. "We don't want to spook our baddie."

From that altitude, they had a fantastic view of the whole area. Almanarre Bay spread out below them, cupped by the thin, curving beach that linked the Giens Peninsula to the mainland. To the east, the Maures Mountains brooded over the rugged coastline. To the west was the naval base of Toulon, backed by Mount Faron, bristling with forts and radar domes.

The pilot tapped Joe's knee. "Highgate is taking off now," he said.

"Roger," Joe replied. He raised his field glasses, scanning the airport. A single-engine plane, silver with a blue stripe, leapt from the end of the runway. Joe felt his breath coming quicker.

To focus himself, he said, "As long as he keeps his distance, we do, too. But if it looks like he's making a run at the sailboard, we move in fast and try to bounce him. Okay?"

"You got it," the pilot said. He seemed to be looking forward to a little excitement.

The small plane took a course that brought it directly under the chopper. Joe brought the binoculars up, trying to make out the face of the mysterious Highgate, but there was too much glare on the windshield to see inside.

The plane banked and began to spiral down toward the water and Frank's sailboard. Joe gripped the armrest of his seat. So far, Highgate didn't seem to be acting aggressively. Had he really meant to attack Doug the day before? He might have come too close by accident. Nothing in this case was quite what it seemed.

At the far side of its spiral, the plane straightened out and the nose tilted down into a power dive aimed directly at the blue-and-red sail.

"This is it," Joe shouted. "Go!"

The chopper pilot pushed the stick forward and gunned the engine. The helicopter roared past Frank, so close overhead that he ducked. Joe held his breath as the chopper headed straight at the oncoming airplane.

Closer, closer. Was Highgate crazy? Had he even noticed them? Just when it seemed impossible to avoid a crash, the single-engine plane swerved wildly.

"Whew," Joe said.

A moment later, his relief turned to horror. Highgate had lost too much altitude in avoiding them. When he banked, his wingtip touched a wave. A burst of spray, and then the blue-and-silver plane was cartwheeling across the water.

White-faced, the helicopter pilot sped toward the downed plane. Frank, on his sailboard, was heading that way, too.

There was no time to waste. The nose and the left wing were under water, and waves washed over the cockpit. The plane was sinking fast.

# 11  Out of the Deep

The chopper swooped low over the sinking airplane. Joe stared down, looking for signs of life. Nothing seemed to be moving in the cockpit. Highgate might be unconscious or even badly injured.

Frank was speeding toward the wreck. When he was a few yards away, he dropped the sail and dove into the water. A moment later he was clambering onto the wing of the plane.

Joe turned to his pilot. "Do you carry a rope ladder?" he demanded.

"Sure. It's in the red box next to the door."

Joe struggled with the door lock, then let the weighted ladder down carefully. Below, Frank tugged at the jammed door of the plane. It opened abruptly, almost throwing him into the water. He leaned inside, then backed out, dragging the pilot behind him. He had to fight to keep his balance as the waves rocked the downed plane. Reaching out, he grasped the ladder, then looked up to give Joe the okay sign.

"A rescue boat is on the way here," the pilot said suddenly. "What do you want to do?"

Joe glanced down. Highgate was already half-way up the ladder, and Frank was right behind him.

"Radio them that we've taken off the only person aboard the plane," he said.

"Roger." The pilot spoke into his microphone, then said, "The authorities want to have a talk with him. They're already waiting at the airport."

Joe reached down to help the dazed Highgate into the helicopter. The man was about thirty, with dark hair and a trim mustache. He looked more like a lawyer than an airborne bad guy.

Joe thought fast. Once the police and the aviation authorities got their hands on Highgate, they wouldn't let a couple of young American investigators see him. This was probably the only chance he and Frank would get to question him.

"Can you make the flight back to the airport as long as possible?" he asked. "We need a little time alone with this guy."

"You bet," the pilot replied. "But no rough stuff, okay? I'm going to have enough questions to answer as it is."

Frank climbed aboard, pulled up the ladder, and swung the door closed.

"Hey," Joe said suddenly, "what about Doug's board?"

"I returned it to its owner," Frank said with a grin. He pointed down at the water. A figure in a distinctive red-and-blue wet suit was swimming with powerful strokes toward the drifting sailboard.

"Okay, buddy," Frank continued, turning to the bedraggled Highgate, "what's the story?"

"What story?" the man blustered. "I was trying to get some pictures of Doug Newman practicing when this madman forced me down."

"You're a photographer? Who do you work for?"

"I'm a free lance."

"Really?" Frank's eyebrows went up. "I suppose you have a business card."

"I don't . . . I'm just starting to break in, I don't have one yet. Hey, what makes you think you can grill me like this?"

Frank and Joe stared at him silently. At first he met their gaze with a look of defiance, but then he dropped his eyes.

"Yesterday you buzzed Doug and knocked him off his board," Frank said. "We have witnesses. And last night, after a fire was set at the Villa Dombray, a note was found threatening Doug if he came out to practice today. He came out anyway. Then you showed up again and dived at his sailboard. Any comments?"

"I don't know anything about a fire," Highgate mumbled. "And I'm sorry about yesterday. It was a mistake. I was trying to get some closeups and I misjudged my distance."

It was time to try a round of good cop/bad cop. "How long have you been here?" Joe asked in a friendly voice. "Where are you staying?"

Highgate turned to him gratefully. "I flew in a couple of days ago," he replied. "I didn't know the town was going to be so jammed with visitors. The only room I could find was at a crummy little hotel a few miles down the coast. I keep forgetting the name of it."

He fumbled around in his jacket pocket and pulled out a card. Another card fluttered to the floor. Highgate reached for it, but Frank got there first.

"'Philip Barstow,'" he read aloud. "'President, Barstow Funboards.' Is he a friend of yours?"

"I never heard of him," Highgate said sullenly. "I don't know how that card got in my pocket."

"Hey, guys," the chopper pilot called. "I'm going to have to set down at the airport now. The gendarmes are starting to get very edgy."

Frank and Joe exchanged a look. It didn't seem that they were going to get much more out of Highgate at this point, anyway.

"Okay," Joe said. "Let's take him in."

After giving carefully vague statements to the

authorities, the Hardys were allowed to leave the airfield. Highgate was still being questioned, but he was sticking to his story about going in too close to the water in order to take photos. It looked as if he would be let off with nothing worse than a fine for reckless flying.

"Okay," Frank said as they drove off. "What are the possibilities? First, Highgate may be just what he says he is, a free-lance photographer and a very careless pilot."

"Fat chance," said Joe.

"I agree. Let's take the other extreme. Is he in back of everything that's been happening at the villa? Do we blame him for the fire, the sabotage, the nighttime incidents?"

Joe frowned. "I don't see how, unless he has an accomplice on the inside. He's never been around there as far as I know."

"What *do* we know about him?" Frank continued. "We know that he buzzed Doug two days in a row. Why?"

"That's easy. He's working for Barstow, who hates Doug for bad-mouthing his sailboards and wants him to lose. And that means Barstow is the inside man. Who would know better how to sabotage a board than a guy who designs them?"

Frank drummed his fingers on the rim of the steering wheel. "Okay," he said thoughtfully. "But why would Barstow sabotage Ian Mitchell's sailboard? Ian may have already agreed to endorse Barstow's new line of products. His endorsement won't be worth much unless he wins."

"It must be a smokescreen," Joe said. "He was trying to confuse us about his real motive."

"If so, it worked," Frank said with a snort. "I'm confused. And we haven't even mentioned the hot sauce in Doug's pasta, or the drawings that disappeared from Dombray's studio, or the counterfeit money."

Joe raised his hands. "Okay, I surrender!"

Frank ignored him. "You know what this case reminds me of? The time Callie's cousin Emily had the flu, tonsillitis, and measles, all at the same time. No one could figure out what it was until they realized that 'it' was more than one thing."

"You mean we might be facing more than one set of bad guys? But if that's so, how do we even know where to start? It's hopeless!"

"Not quite," Frank replied. "What we have to do is go back over everything that's happened and try to figure out who or what the target was. With Highgate, that's easy: his target both times was Doug. But what about the falling tiles? Doug again? Or us? Or maybe anyone who happened to be walking by at the wrong time?"

"I get it," said Joe. "So whoever sabotaged the mast mounts might have been aiming at Doug and Ian or might not even have cared whose boards he damaged."

"Uh-huh. And the floor wax at the head of the stairs must have been aimed at whoever happened to come along first."

"But why would anyone want to hurt people randomly like that? What's his motive?"

"I don't know," Frank said slowly. "But I have a hunch that once we figure that out, we'll know who's behind it as well."

The Hardys returned to the villa to find Doug with Catherine in her office. They quickly filled them in on what had happened at the airport.

"Highgate wasn't arrested, then?" Doug said.

"Not as far as we know," Joe replied. "We left before him, but it didn't look as though they were going to give him too much grief."

"Good," Doug said. "Maybe you're surprised I feel that way, but after all, he didn't hurt anyone, and maybe he really is a photographer."

Frank shrugged. "Maybe, but I hope the next time he decides to take some aerial shots, he finds someone else to pilot the plane for him. Oh, one funny thing: he had Philip Barstow's business card in his pocket."

"Barstow?" Doug exclaimed. "That creep! I knew it!"

"Of course it doesn't prove anything— Barstow could have given him the card for lots of reasons—but it does make me want to ask Barstow a few questions."

"Too late," said Catherine. "He brought in a

van this morning, loaded all his equipment, and drove away. I asked him where he was going, but he refused to tell me. He said he was afraid that my bad luck might follow him."

"We'll track him down," Joe said. "He's bound to show up at the meet tomorrow."

Catherine smiled and shook her head. "It doesn't matter. Now I know that *he* was my 'bad luck,' and thanks to you and Frank, he has been scared away. From now on, the Villa Dombray will be a happier place. And to celebrate, we shall have a very special feast for everyone tonight!"

Frank started to say that it was a little too soon to celebrate. Then he looked at Catherine's beaming face and kept his mouth shut. After all, she might be right. And if she wasn't, they would find out soon enough.

Joe looked around the buzzing dining room. Everyone had made an effort to dress up, for Catherine's sake, and everyone was enjoying the wonderful French meal. It had started with thin slices of spicy country sausage and tiny, sharp pickles, followed by omelets with mushrooms and an herb Joe didn't recognize.

He was already starting to feel full when the main course arrived: sliced chicken and artichoke hearts in a creamy sauce. He had never liked the way artichokes look, but Catherine was sitting

107

just down the table from him and he had to try the dish. Once he tasted it, he kept going until he had cleaned his plate.

He sighed and pushed his chair back, almost bumping into one of the life-size marble statues that lined the room.

"Don't relax yet," Doug said from across the table. "We still have dessert and cheeses to come." He smiled maliciously at Joe's expression of dismay.

"Do you always train for a meet this way?" Joe returned.

"I'm going to try to from now on. After all, the more weight you can put on the boom, the faster you can go."

"Unless you get so heavy you sink," Ian said from the next table. The open hostility in his voice made a silence fall over the room.

Catherine quickly stood up and lifted her glass. "Friends," she said, "tomorrow is the day you have all been waiting and training for. It has been a real pleasure for me to have all of you here with me at the Villa Dombray. My only regret is that my uncle could not have lived long enough to watch once more the wonderful sport he loved so much. If he had, I know he would join me in wishing you—*all* of you—the very best of luck tomorrow."

Like everyone else in the room, Frank stood up to applaud their hostess. Then something caught his eye, something so strange that he had a hard time believing it. The marble statue of a Roman soldier just behind Catherine seemed to be teetering back and forth, apparently on its own.

Was it a trick of the light? No, others saw it and gasped.

Then the statue began to fall directly toward Catherine, ready to crush her under its weight!

# 12 I Accuse . . .

"Catherine," Frank shouted. "Look out!"

The marble statue was toppling, and Catherine was directly in its path. Frank leapt at her and pulled her to the floor, but before he could drag her out of danger, the head and shoulders of the statue smashed into the table. Dishes and glasses shattered. The tip of the spear in the statue's hand broke off and flew across the room.

"Catherine! Frank!"

Joe pulled the remains of a chair out of his way and knelt down next to the table. He dreaded what he might see. The statue certainly weighed hundreds of pounds, and anyone in its way must have been badly injured, or worse.

"Here," Frank's voice said. "Help us out of here, quick!"

Joe stared. Frank and Catherine were huddled under the table, next to the thick central pillar. The tabletop was still holding the weight of the statue, but it was starting to creak ominously. Joe crawled quickly under the table and helped his brother pull Catherine to safety. A moment later came the noise of splintering wood, and the battered statue crashed to the floor.

"Catherine! Are you all right?" Doug demanded. "Are you hurt?" He took her arm and helped her to her feet.

She didn't answer. She stared in shock at the ruins of the table.

"We must all leave this place at once," a voice said loudly. Joe looked around. Emil Molitor was standing on a bench on the other side of the room, addressing a little huddle of shaken windsurfers.

"It is not safe to stay here any longer," he continued. "We were told that the person responsible for all these accidents had left, that all would now be well. But you see that that is not true. Whatever is behind these events, whether it is an evil person or something else, we are all in danger as long as we remain here."

"Bull," Doug called out. "All we have to do is find out who's behind it and put *him* behind something, like bars!"

"But you saw the statue fall," Emil replied. "Who made it fall? Who was near it? No one!"

"Interesting, isn't it?" Frank said. "How could a heavy piece of marble like that topple over, all on its own?"

He went over to the place where the statue had

111

been and got down on one knee. When he stood up, he was holding a heavy metal wedge in his hand.

"This was on the floor, near the wall," he said. Everyone moved in closer to listen. "There's also a big pool of water on the floor."

"Maybe it spilled when the statue hit the table," someone said.

"Maybe," Frank said. "But maybe when it was put there it wasn't water."

After a moment of puzzled silence, Doug said, "Ice!"

Frank smiled. "That's my hunch," he said. "Someone put this wedge under the back of the statue, then leveled the statue out again with a block of ice under the front edge. Once the ice melted, the statue was unbalanced and it fell over."

Frank waited for everyone to digest the idea before continuing. "And this time we can be pretty sure that it *isn't* Philip Barstow. He left the villa this morning, and this booby trap must have been set in the last couple of hours."

"Then . . ." Catherine turned to face Ian. "It's you, isn't it, Ian? I've tried not to believe it, I've tried for days now. But it's time for me to face the truth."

Her former boyfriend was pale. "Cathy—" he began.

"I thought I knew you," she went on. Tears glistened in her eyes. "What did I know? I knew you were jealous of Doug, I knew you were angry at both of us. But I never thought you would come to hate me. I never thought you would try to kill me."

"But I didn't," he said. He, too, sounded near tears. "I never did. All I—"

Doug elbowed his way through the crowd and grabbed Ian's shirtfront. "Liar," he shouted. "You're the one who's been trying to ruin the inn! Who else would want to hurt Catherine by ruining her business!"

The crowd of boardsailors, all of them friends of Catherine's, let out an angry growl and moved closer.

Doug cocked his fist, ready to punch his rival in the face. Joe moved in to break up the fight, but before he could act, Ian twisted free and gave Doug a powerful push. Doug staggered backward and stumbled over Joe's foot. As he fell to the floor, Ian darted out of the dining room.

"Stop him, someone!" Catherine cried. "Please, stop him before somebody gets hurt!"

Joe and Frank ran out of the room, closely followed by Doug and half a dozen others. The living room was empty, but from the stairwell came the sound of pounding feet.

"Come on," Frank shouted, taking the steps two at a time. At the head of the stairs he paused and quickly looked both ways. The hallway was empty. Not a sound, not a sign of life.

"You take the rooms on this floor," he said

113

quietly to Joe, who was right behind him. "I'll try upstairs."

"Right," Joe replied. "Come on, you guys. He can't get away!"

"I'll watch the stairs," Doug said loudly. "And he'd better not try to get by me if he wants to stay in one piece!"

Frank ran silently up the stairs to the third floor. All the doors along the hallway were closed. He tried the one just opposite the head of the stairs. The room contained a bed, a mirror-topped dresser, and a white wicker chair. A wildly patterned wet suit in purple, green, and black had been tossed on the chair. Frank glanced around and closed the door.

The next door to the left led to the broom closet. Nothing there but brooms and cleaning supplies. He tried the other doors at that end of the hall, but all of them were locked. He stopped and considered. Had Ian had enough time to run into one of the rooms and lock the door behind him? If so, searching the rooms was going to mean getting a master key from Catherine. If there was one.

Frank shook his head. The door latches were old and noisy. He couldn't be positive, but he thought he would have heard the click if Ian had fastened one of the locks. So it wasn't too likely that he was hiding in one of the locked rooms. And judging by the frustration in the voices from the floor below, he hadn't been found there, either. So where was he?

Frank took another look up and down the hall. Time to try the doors in the other direction. Passing the door at the head of the stairs, he noticed that he hadn't closed it all the way. He grasped the knob and started to pull the door shut. Then, through the crack, he saw that the purple and green wet suit was now lying on the floor. Someone had moved it!

He flung the door open, just in time to see a figure slip through the glass doors onto the balcony. It was Ian.

"Hold it," Frank shouted.

Ian grabbed a flowerpot from the floor of the balcony and hurled it at Frank, who dove out of the way. The pot shattered against the door, and dirt rained down on Frank's head. By the time he wiped it from his eyes, Ian was at the far end of the balcony.

"Ian, wait!" Frank shouted again, then gasped as Ian put both hands on the balcony railing and did a perfect forward flip, let go of the railing, and vanished.

Frank rushed onto the balcony and stared down into the darkness. The stone terrace was over thirty feet below. Ian couldn't possibly have survived a fall like that. But among the shadowy forms on the terrace, there was nothing that looked like a body. Where—?

Frank grasped the railing and leaned as far out as he could. There was another balcony just under the one he was standing on. He couldn't see much of it from that angle, but in the corner was something that looked like the toe of a shoe. Unless the room's occupant was in the habit of leaving his shoes on the balcony, it had to be Ian who was crouching there.

Frank took a deep breath and climbed over the railing. The ground was a long way down. The wrought-iron railing bit into his fingers as he let himself down the full length of his arms. He brought his feet up and swung them forward. It was now or never. Releasing his hold on the railing, he fell toward the balcony below. The railing struck him in the small of the back, and he felt himself start to topple over. Then strong hands grabbed his shirt and pulled him to safety.

Frank took another deep breath and said, "Thanks."

"Don't bother thanking me," Ian said gloomily. "The balcony door is locked. I couldn't have gotten away even if I'd let you fall."

Inside, the ceiling light came on. Joe, Doug, and half a dozen others rushed into the room and unlocked the doors to the balcony.

"Don't try anything, Ian," Doug said, his fists clenched. "You can't escape this time!"

# 13 At Bay at Last

Ian sat slumped over in his chair. His shoulders sagged, and his chin was resting on his chest.

"How many times do I have to tell you?" he asked in a tired voice. "I didn't wreck anybody's board, I didn't try to hurt Cathy with that statue, and I don't know anybody named Highgate. The only thing I did was sneak a big gob of hot sauce into Doug's spaghetti."

"You knew about all the harassment that was going on," said Frank. "Your own sailboard had been tampered with. Why did you add to it by doctoring Doug's food?"

Ian shrugged. "I don't know, it seemed very funny at the time. I didn't plan to do it. But Doug was always mouthing off about his secret diet tricks. There was his plate of pasta, and there was the dish of hot sauce. It was a natural."

Doug, Catherine, and three others who were staying at the inn were in chairs on the far side of

117

the room. The Hardys would rather have questioned Ian in private, but Catherine had insisted. All of them had been victims of the jinx, she'd said, and all of them had a right to know what was going on. The Hardys had finally agreed, on condition that the observers keep their mouths closed.

Joe stirred in his chair. "If you're as innocent as you say, why did you run away tonight?"

"Something snapped, that's all," Ian replied. "It shook me up when that statue fell over and nearly hit Cathy. And then she accused me like that, staring at me as if I were a piece of dirt. The way everybody started crowding around, I thought they were about to lynch me. I had to get away."

Joe and Frank exchanged a long glance. They had been questioning Ian for over half an hour now, and he hadn't changed his responses or tripped over a detail once. Either he was telling the truth or he had constructed an airtight story. And either way, they wouldn't gain anything by going over the same ground again and again. It was time for a change of tactics.

Frank stood up. "Okay," he said. "All we can do now is call the police."

Catherine too was on her feet. "The police?" she repeated. "But why? All he did was play a joke in bad taste. That's not something to call the police about."

"I agree about the cops," Doug said, "but I don't swallow Ian's story for a minute. What about that statue tonight, was that just a joke? You could have been killed!"

"But we have no reason to think that Ian was responsible," she replied. "It could have been anyone. Even the police will understand that."

She turned back to Frank and Joe. "Isn't there any way to avoid turning Ian over to the police?"

"Sorry," Joe said, shaking his head. "They'll be able to track down his links to Highgate, for one thing. We don't have the facilities for that kind of investigation."

"Now wait a minute," Doug began.

Catherine broke in. "The meet!" she said. "The meet is tomorrow. If the police hold Ian even for a day, he will miss the meet!"

"He should have thought of that earlier," said Frank. He reached across the desk for the telephone.

"Well, Doug," said Ian bitterly. "Congratulations. I guess you get to keep the Almanarre Cup after all. I just hope every time you look at it, you remember how you won it. You'd better believe everybody else will."

"Stop!" Catherine cried. "Stop it! Frank, Joe, please, you mustn't do this. I don't care about the villa. Maybe it *is* jinxed. I'll give it up. I'll sell it to Emil to become a museum. But I will not let our lives be ruined this way."

119

She turned to Doug. "You understand, don't you? Ian is right, we would always remember, and it would poison us."

"Stop it, Catherine!" Doug stood up and looked around the room as if he had never seen this place or these people before in his life.

"I—I want you to meet Tom Highgate's best client. Me!"

Joe and Frank exchanged a look of weary satisfaction. Doug had just confirmed their hunch.

"Highgate?" said Catherine. "Doug, I don't understand. What are you saying?"

"It's not that complicated," he replied. "A few months ago a guy came to me and said he wanted to represent me. It was Tom Highgate. I'd never thought I needed a sports rep before, but windsurfing is changing fast. Too fast to keep up with. Besides, Tom used to be with one of the sports networks and he knows a bunch of important TV people. So I said yes."

"But why—" Catherine started to ask.

"He caught me at a time that I was starting to feel a little panicked," Doug continued. "I know I can't stay king of the mountain much longer. There are a lot of young kids coming up who've been windsurfing since they got out of diapers. They'll be blowing my doors off before long."

He glanced over at his rival and said, "Don't grin, Ian. You're just a year younger than I am. You don't have that long left, either."

Ian shrugged. "I'll worry about that next year."

"Anyway, Tom came up with a plan. Winning the Almanarre Cup for the third time would be a very big thing, maybe the biggest in my career. But it wouldn't make that much difference unless it got media exposure—a *lot* of it. What if it looked like somebody was out to stop me from winning the Cup? The media would eat it up. They'd turn me into a star.

"He was right, too. I heard today that camera teams have shown up from two networks that hadn't been planning to cover the meet at all."

He paused. "Tom's a little kooky, though. He gets weird ideas, like renting that airplane and buzzing me while I was out practicing. He nearly killed himself doing it."

"Not to mention me," Frank said quietly.

"Yeah, I know. I'm sorry. When you sprang that scheme of yours on me this morning, I tried to think of some way of getting out of it, but you had me in a corner. I left a message at Tom's hotel, telling him to call it off, and when I called back they said they'd given the message to him. I figured we were all right. When I saw that airplane show up anyway, I felt sick. Did you know about him and me already?"

"We suspected," Frank replied. "The press was finding out about these incidents a little too quickly. Somebody had to be keeping them informed, and that spelled publicity stunt."

Catherine shook her head in disbelief. "Doug,

I don't understand. You mean that you and this Highgate person put us through all this worry and almost destroyed my business just to get a little publicity? How could you!"

"But I didn't! *We* didn't! Sure, Tom buzzed me with that plane, and he made sure the reporters knew about the so-called campaign against me. He dreamed up that threatening note, too, but that was all. He didn't tamper with our sailboards, or set the fire last night, or do anything to the statue. I swear he didn't, and neither did I!"

"Neither did I," Ian said.

Joe frowned. "Doug, what about the time you fell asleep at the wheel, bringing us back from the airport?"

"Yeah," Ian added, "and accused me of doping your tomato juice!"

Doug stared down at his hands. "Orange juice," he said. "And I really did think you'd done it, Ian. Now I'm not so sure. When I started to take a hay fever tablet this morning, I saw that some of them were different from the rest. My guess is that they're more powerful and that that's what put me out."

He looked up and met Catherine's eyes. "Is there any way you can understand?" he pleaded. "Can you ever forgive me for not telling you sooner?"

She looked away. "I—I don't know," she said softly. "I will try."

"And the rest of you? I'm sorry I let you down."

There was an awkward silence. Then, to everyone's surprise, Ian said, "Forget it, Dougie. All of us do stupid things now and then. Sometimes really stupid—like that hot sauce I put in your pasta. This business of yours with Highgate was a real bonehead move, but it's past. The important thing is the meet tomorrow."

Doug shook his head. "I'm pulling out," he said. "After all that's happened, I don't have any right to compete."

"Oh, no, you don't," Ian said. "You think I want people to say that the only reason I won the Almanarre Cup was because you quit? No way, my man! We can't have a contest without you— somebody has to finish in second place!"

Doug stared at his longtime rival without speaking. Finally he said, "Okay, Ian, I'll be there tomorrow. But don't get too used to talking about me and second place in the same sentence."

"We'll see about that," replied Ian, getting to his feet. "Come on, you guys. If we don't bag some Zs, we might fall asleep on the starting line tomorrow."

Catherine said good night to Doug and stayed behind to talk with Joe and Frank. "Now we know who has been after Doug," she said. "But who is to blame for the falling statue? And all the rest? That's still a mystery, isn't it?"

"It sure is," Frank replied. "A double mystery, in a way—I can't see how someone working alone could have managed to move the statue. It's too heavy."

"And remember last night?" Joe added. "The guy I was chasing got away in a boat, and meanwhile somebody else set that fire in the shed."

"It's horrible," said Catherine. "I feel as if I'm surrounded by enemies without faces. And I don't even know what they want of me. Why would anyone risk killing a complete stranger by pushing a heavy bundle of tiles off the roof!"

"We don't know why yet," Joe said, "but after tonight we know how. Remember the puddle of water on the scaffold? Our bad guys must have used the same melting-ice trick with the tiles. That's why we didn't find anyone up there when we searched."

Frank scowled. "Right, but . . . Look, the statue must have been rigged like that to make us think there really was a sinister curse on the villa. But why rig the tiles that way? Especially since there was no way of knowing exactly how long the ice would take to melt or whether anybody would be underneath when the tiles finally fell?"

"The only thing I can think of," Joe said, "is that whoever did it wanted to be somewhere else when the tiles fell, to have an alibi. But that can't be right. None of the people we talked to claimed to have an alibi, anyway."

"I'm getting a headache from all these puzzles," Catherine said. "And from staying too long in this room. Look, the moon is up. Why not step outside for some fresh air?"

"Good idea," Frank replied.

Catherine opened the glass doors that led onto the terrace. "Watch where you step," she warned. "The workmen who are repairing the roof have left some of their equipment on the terrace."

Joe and Frank followed her outside. It was another beautiful night. The wind had died down to a gentle breeze that carried the scent of flowers to where they stood. The moon seemed brighter, casting a pool of light on the whole bay. Across the water, lights twinkled in the cottages on the peninsula.

Joe shuddered. He couldn't look at the sky without remembering those awful moments clinging to the bush, feeling it pull loose from the soil, and wondering if Frank would get to him in time. He took a step backward.

"Ouch! Who left a ladder here?"

"I'm sorry," said Catherine. "I did warn you. It was not nice of the men to leave it in the way, but I do not feel I can complain. They are charging me much less than I expected to have to pay."

"No, it's my fault," Joe said. "I didn't look."

For a moment he was silent. Then he added in a

casual voice, "By the way, where do those guys come from? The ones who are working on the roof? Some company in town?"

"Oh, no, Emil found them for me. I think he had used them before to do work for him. He has been so helpful to me in so many ways. I do not know what I would have done without him."

Joe glanced over at Frank, who looked like he was having some of the same thoughts. They were still a little short on answers, but it looked as if they were beginning to find some of the right questions.

# 14 Fight to the Finish

Joe pushed his way through the crowd to where Frank was standing. "Here," he said, handing him a bottle of orange soda. "This will cool you off."

The Hardys had been at Almanarre Beach since early morning, watching the preliminary heats of the match. Doug had won all his easily, and so had Ian. It looked like a sure thing that the two rivals would face off in the final for the Cup.

"Excuse me, folks, make way there!" A three-person camera crew was making its way down to the water's edge, where Doug was checking over his rig and trading jokes with some of his fans. This was the fifth or sixth camera crew that Joe and Frank had seen so far.

"Looks like Highgate does good work," Frank

observed. "The media are really out in force today."

"Yeah," Joe replied. "And it looks like they're going to turn Doug into a star, too—if he wins. Hey, why do you suppose Highgate had Philip Barstow's card in his pocket, if Barstow didn't have anything to do with harassing Doug?"

Frank smiled. "Highgate's a sports rep. He makes his living cutting deals for the guys he represents, especially endorsement and sponsorship deals with manufacturers. And Barstow's a manufacturer."

"But there's no way Doug is going to endorse Barstow's boards. He thinks they're crummy!"

Frank's smile grew broader. "Sure," he replied. "But who says Doug is the only windsurfer Highgate hopes to sign up? Here he comes, by the way."

Highgate stopped in front of them, his hands in his pockets. He looked upset and angry.

"Do you know how much you guys cost me?" he demanded. "I'm going to have to pay a big fine and part of the cost of that plane you forced down, not to mention what I spent just getting over here. And now Doug says he's pulling out of our deal. I don't even have a client, and it's all your fault!"

"It's your own fault," Frank said calmly. "If you had stuck to representing Doug honestly, instead of dreaming up crooked publicity stunts, you'd be down there right now, helping him with his interviews for worldwide television."

Highgate glared at him. For a moment he looked tempted to throw a punch. Instead he said, "I'll remember you guys." Without waiting for a reply, he spun around and strode off along the beach.

"Same here," Joe called after him.

Frank glanced at his wrist. "We've got some time before the next heat," he said. "Why don't we walk over to the pavilion and get a look at the Almanarre Cup? After all, it's practically at the center of this case."

The Almanarre Cup had been taken out of the bank vault that morning. Now it was on display in an open-sided tent at the head of the beach. The Hardys joined the line of people waiting for a chance to look at the famous trophy.

The silver cup was resting on a pedestal draped with black velvet. Spotlights in the four corners of the tent drew blinding highlights from the polished surface of the engraved silver. A red velvet rope kept the spectators at a safe distance, and a uniformed guard watched to make sure that no one stepped across the barrier.

"Look at that," Frank said in a low voice. "The scene on the side of the bowl—that's Almanarre Bay. You can almost pick out the spot we're standing on. It's hard to believe that anyone could engrave something so realistically."

"That's nothing," replied Joe. "Take a close look at the figure of a windsurfer on the top of the bowl. Does it remind you of anybody?"

Frank stared. "Of course," he exclaimed. "It's Doug! Not exactly, of course, but anybody who knows him well would see the resemblance. I remember he said he modeled for Dombray, but I didn't know it was for the Almanarre Cup. No wonder he's so determined to win it!"

The loudspeakers were announcing the final heat of the wave competition, the heat that would decide the winner of the Almanarre Cup. As Frank had predicted, and as a lot of the spectators had hoped, the heat matched Doug Newman and Ian Mitchell.

The Hardys found Catherine near the judges' stand. Just below them, the television crews were politely jostling each other for the best filming spots.

"How is Doug feeling?" Joe asked Catherine.

"Good. Earlier he was afraid that all these distractions had made him lose his edge," she replied. "Not now, though. Once he starts competing and hits his stride, he starts to feel that he is bound to win. Today is the same. He knows that Ian is very, very good, almost as good as he is—even better some days. But he is convinced that no one can beat him today."

"Let's hope he's right," Frank said. "It'd be a real blow if he lost."

"He *will* lose . . . someday. But not today."

Doug and Ian were already on their boards, warming up just south of the observation zone. The conditions in the bay were nearly perfect, with a three-foot swell and a steady fifteen-to-twenty-knot wind from the north.

Catherine jumped as the starting gun blasted just behind her. Moments later the two windsurfers were crossing into the observation zone. The crowd gasped as Doug blasted off the lip of a wave into a loop, then cheered as Ian followed him into the air. Moments later Doug was performing a barrel roll. Once more Ian followed him move for move. It was as if they had rehearsed together for weeks. Then they were past the zone of observation and turning for the next run.

This time Doug started off by showing his wave-riding skills, while Ian gave the cheering crowd another barrel roll. But no sooner had Ian found a soft spot to land than Doug was launching his board into a perfect forward roll. It looked as if he were waiting calmly in midair while the earth spun under him.

"Five and a half minutes," Catherine said tensely. "Four and a half to go."

The thousands watching from the beach, and the millions who later watched the films on television, saw a stunning display of style and control. Ian and Doug were throwing every roll and aerial in the book, and a few too new to be in

131

the book, and they were hitting every time. Most of the spectators were silent now, as if they were holding their breath for the conclusion.

Catherine grabbed Frank's arm and squeezed it hard. Doug had just come off the lip of a particularly strong wave and started what looked like a loop. But instead of finishing it the usual way, he paused with the bottom of his board pointing at the sky and his sail parallel to the water. He was suspended from the foot straps and the wishbone, and he looked as if he had just discovered the secret of turning a sailboard into a hang glider.

The nose of the board tilted down. Frank held his breath. In another instant the board was going to hit the water, with Doug underneath. Was he going to have to be pulled out, in the last round of the most important meet of his life, with all those TV cameras aimed at him? He would never live it down.

Then, in a move too quick to follow, the sail was catching the wind again and the board righted itself, just as the next wave rose up to meet it. In a fan-shaped burst of spray, Doug was gliding quickly out of the observation zone. A moment later, the final gun sounded. The heat was finished.

The crowd went wild. Even those who knew nothing about the sport realized that they had just seen something remarkable. As Doug sailed in and beached his board, other competitors gathered around to slap his back and shake his hand. Ian was getting his share of attention, too. He had turned in a nearly perfect round that lacked only the flair of Doug's final maneuver.

The loudspeakers crackled. The crowd fell silent. "In the master wave competition for the Almanarre Cup, the decision of the judges is as follows: Ian Mitchell, wave riding, ten points; jumps, eight points; reentries, ten points."

Joe looked at Frank wide-eyed. It was almost unheard-of for a competitor to be awarded a score of twenty-eight out of thirty.

"Doug Newman," the voice continued, "wave riding, nine points; jumps, ten points; reentries, nine points."

A tense, puzzled silence settled over the crowd.

"The two finalists are tied at twenty-eight points each," the announcer explained. "The rules state that, in the case of such a tie, the winner is the competitor with the higher score in the jumps. Accordingly, the judges have declared that the winner of this year's competition, and of the Almanarre Cup, is Doug Newman."

Catherine rushed down the beach and pushed her way through the cheering crowd. She had just enough time to stammer her congratulations. Then four of the other boardsailors grabbed Doug by the hands and feet, swung him high into the air, and threw him far out into the surf. He staggered to his feet sputtering and laughing.

"Great work, Doug," Frank said when he could work his way close enough to the new winner.

"Yeah, fantastic," Joe added.

"Thanks to you guys," Doug said. Then he looked more closely at them and a devilish grin took over his face.

"Hey, Ian," he shouted. "Did you see these dudes? They're bone-dry!"

"Now, wait a minute," Frank began. It was too late. A moment later, as the crowd of surfers roared with laughter, he and Joe were being tossed into the waves.

"I think we're members of the club now," Frank said to Joe as they waded ashore.

"Super," Joe replied, looking down at his soaked leather running shoes, "but I'm not sure I can afford the dues."

As the spectators began to make their way back to their cars or changed into suits for a late-afternoon swim, Joe saw Catherine standing near a pile of baskets and cartons. She seemed to be looking for someone. When she noticed Joe and Frank, she beckoned them over.

"Tonight I'm giving a party right here on the beach," she announced. "We'll build a fire of driftwood and prepare a wonderful soup called bouillabaisse, with ten different kinds of fish. William is going back to the villa to get everything we need."

Joe wasn't sure how he felt about fish soup, however many different kinds of fish went into it.

Then he had an idea. "Say, Catherine, how about we roast some wienies on the fire, too? We can get mustard and pickles and buns, and even throw in some potato chips. Our treat," he added. "Right, Frank?"

"Uh, sure," Frank said, pulling out his wallet to check on his supply of cash. "How many people are you expecting to come to this party?"

"About fifty, I think," Catherine replied. "I am expecting—"

But Frank wasn't listening. He was staring down at the bank note in his hand. "Joe," he said urgently. "The man's picture on this bill—I knew I'd seen it before. It's exactly the same face as in that drawing I saw in the studio. The one that vanished!"

Joe grabbed the bill from Frank's hand and stared at it in turn. "Are you sure?" he demanded. "But what—"

"*Help! Help!*"

The Hardys spun around. The shouts were coming from the pavilion. They ran up the beach, dodging around little knots of spectators, and dashed into the open tent.

The guard was lying on the ground, holding the side of his head. The four spotlights still shone down on the center of the tent, but the velvet-draped pedestal was empty. The Almanarre Cup was gone!

# 15 A Race for the Prize

"I don't get it!" Doug nibbled at the tip of his thumb and stared across the terrace at the bay. "Run that by me again. What did the cops say?"

Frank looked down at the notes he had taken during his brief phone call with the commander of the local gendarmes.

"As soon as the theft was discovered, they set up roadblocks on both highways that lead away from the beach," he repeated. "There was already a big traffic jam on those roads, so the thieves couldn't have escaped before the roadblocks went up. They checked out every single car that left Almanarre Beach this afternoon—thousands of them."

"And zip," Doug said bitterly.

Frank nodded. "They also had a helicopter

watching the bay. The Cup was not taken off by boat."

"So either the thief carried it off on foot," said Joe, "or it's still in the area."

"Thieves," Frank said. "The guard is positive that he was attacked by two men. Anyway, the commandant couldn't keep the area sealed off any longer. A forest fire has been spotted a few miles east of here, and he needs every man he's got. The roadblocks came down about ten minutes ago."

"That's it, then," Doug said. "The Cup's gone for good. Funny—one minute I was on top of the world. I had everything I'd hoped for. And a minute later . . ."

Catherine took his arm. "Is the Cup so important to you?" she asked softly. "Everyone knows that you won it. Whether you have the Cup or not, you still have that."

"I know, I know, but . . . It's hard to explain. Winning the Almanarre Cup should have been the high point of my career, like a runner inning a gold medal in the Olympics. And this afternoon really felt like my personal best. I don't know if I'll ever be able to perform that well again in competition."

"Sure you will," Ian said from the other side of the terrace. "I wish I didn't think so—I'd like to beat you at least once before we hang up our wet suits!"

Doug grinned for a moment, then his face became somber again. "Whether I do or not," he went on, "the Cup was the symbol of what I'd done. And now I've lost it."

"We'll get it back," Frank said. "You have our word on it."

"I wish I could believe that. But by now it's probably been melted down."

The idea of someone destroying her late uncle's masterpiece made Catherine gasp.

"I don't think so," Frank said quickly. "Oh, sure, the silver in the Cup is worth a lot of money, but that's not what the crooks are after. I think they want the Cup because it can tell them something they need to know."

"What?" Doug exclaimed. "How can the Cup tell them anything?"

"What Frank means—" Joe began. But Frank grabbed his arm and pointed toward the driveway.

The two roofers had just come out of the house and were carrying a big carton to their van.

"They worked awfully late tonight, didn't they?" Frank said quietly. "Interesting, how they kept on until after the police roadblocks were taken down. I wouldn't mind knowing what they're carrying in that box."

"You don't think . . . ?"

"Oh, yes, I do! Come on!"

The Hardys dashed across the terrace and down the steps to the parking area. The roofer in the beret saw them coming and said something to his companion. The two ran for the doors of the van and scrambled into the front seat.

"Hold it!" Joe shouted. Then he and Frank had to leap aside to keep from being run over. Gravel spurted from under the wheels as the van roared up the drive and made a tire-squealing left turn onto the highway.

"The motorcycles," Frank cried. "Quick!"

Joe ran for the nearer of the bikes and grabbed the helmet off the seat. He had his fingers crossed that the key would be in the ignition as usual. It was. He pushed the heavy, powerful machine off its kickstand, forked it, and turned the key. The motor fired instantly. He released the clutch, twisted the throttle, and fishtailed up the driveway. Frank was right behind him.

A truck was laboring up the hill as they reached the road. No time to weigh the odds. Once they let the van get out of sight for long, the game was finished. Joe gunned the motorcycle. A horn blared as he roared past the front of the truck and slid into the far lane. He had just enough time to see the startled truck driver shake a fist at him, then he was leaning far over and guiding the bike around the next curve.

For a short stretch the road straightened out. Joe opened the throttle all the way. There were four or five vehicles in sight ahead of him. He squinted, trying to make out details, but the light of the setting sun on his visor blurred everything.

Was that the van just going around the next curve?

Frank pulled up next to him and pointed. His bike seemed a little faster, and Joe motioned for him to go ahead, but Frank shook his head and stayed alongside. A moment later they were snaking through a series of curves that brought them out onto a steep hillside overlooking the sea.

There was no time to enjoy the scenery. They passed one car, then another, but suddenly they had a battered old sedan in front of them, chugging up the slope in a cloud of oily smoke. An oncoming bus filled the other lane, followed by a long line of impatient cars.

As he grabbed the brakes, Joe saw their quarry vanishing around the next curve. What could he do? The narrow road didn't leave him room to pass, unless . . . Just over the next rise he saw a sign for a service station. If only—he motioned for Frank to drop back and give him room to maneuver. A moment later he swerved into the entrance of the station, roared past the pumps, and slid back onto the road two car lengths ahead of the old clunker.

He bent over the handlebars, almost hugging the gas tank to cut his wind resistance and gain speed. The speedometer needle climbed past the 100 mark to 120, then 130. He had to remind himself that that was kilometers per hour and not miles. He was really going only 85 miles an hour or so, but on a winding mountain road that was fast enough.

Or was it? Where was the van? He should have caught up to it by now. On the next straight stretch, he stared hopefully, but the road was empty. The only sign of life was a handful of cars in the parking area of a roadside vegetable stand.

Cars . . . and a van! He and Frank were a couple of hundred yards past the stand before they realized what they had seen. Braking hard, they skidded around and roared back toward the stand. At that moment, a big black sedan pulled out of the lot and headed toward them—*straight* toward them!

"Look out!" Joe screamed, though he knew his brother couldn't hear him.

The powerful car filled the center of the road. Joe dodged to the left, toward the shoulder, and felt his rear wheel start to break away. Frantically he twisted the handlebars in the direction of the skid and fought to stay upright. For a moment he was sure that he was about to slide under the wheels of the oncoming car. Then his tires found a grip on the road and he was able to steer around his attacker and stop.

Frank wasn't so lucky. The driver of the black car chose him as his next target. Frank tried to dodge to the right, but the car moved over still more, leaving him zero room. He swerved onto the shoulder. The moment the bike hit the loose gravel, it went into a skid. Frank bailed out. Tucking his head, elbows, and knees, he rolled helplessly down a short, brush-covered slope and lay still.

"Frank!" Joe came running down the slope. "Frank! Are you okay?"

Frank sat up cautiously. "Nothing's broken," he said. "But I've got enough scratches and bruises to last me a while. What about my bike?"

"We'll check it out later. Come on!"

They scrambled up the slope to the road and Joe's bike. Frank climbed on behind and they took off in pursuit of the murderous sedan.

Joe slowed down for a sharp bend. As they came out of it, they could see a whole sweep of cliffs falling to the water. A line of white railings showed the twisting path of the highway as it climbed toward the top.

"There," Frank shouted, and pointed ahead. The black sedan was just across the inlet from them, speeding up the road. Joe twisted the throttle and tried to squeeze another ounce of power from the roaring engine. He could see far enough ahead to use the whole road. They swooped around the curves, one after another, canting over so far that the foot guards touched the pavement, casting up showers of sparks.

Suddenly they rounded a curve and found the black sedan right in front of them. One of the workmen was staring out the back window, his mouth moving. He had a cigarette glued to his lower lip. Joe pulled out and came alongside, but the car swerved wildly in their direction. He had to brake to keep from being forced over the side of the cliff.

He fell back. What good would it do to pass the car? As long as he kept them in sight, the crooks couldn't escape. By now Doug and Catherine must have alerted the authorities. At any moment the gendarmes would be joining the chase.

The driver of the car must have realized that this was his last chance to get away. He sped up, driving more and more recklessly, taking crazy chances on the curves. The big car veered from one side of the road to the other.

The road dipped into a little wooded valley. At the bottom was a small, one-lane bridge over a deep, shadowy ravine. The car roared down toward the bridge just as a tractor started across from the other side. The tractor driver looked up with a horrified expression and jumped for his life onto the roadway, leaving his tractor stalled in the middle of the bridge.

The black car swerved wildly. Tires screaming, it lurched, spun around, and slammed sideways into the concrete wall of the bridge. A cloud of steam rose from the crumpled hood.

Joe brought the motorcycle to a halt a few feet away. He and Frank rushed over to the battered car. They forced open the doors and pulled out the occupants. The two workmen were too dazed from the crash to put up a fight.

The last to come out was the driver, the king-pin of the gang. Frank and Joe stared at him grimly for a long moment. Then, as they heard the distant *pam-pom* of an approaching police car, Frank said, "It looks as if that jinx has finally turned on you, Mister Molitor."

# 16 The Villain Unmasked

"Emil?" Catherine said.

She looked around the living room as if she had suddenly found herself in a strange new place.

"I still can't believe it. He was my uncle's best friend!"

"Not such a good friend," said Frank. "He's told the whole story to the gendarmes. As your uncle's agent, he swindled him for years, claiming that the money had been lost in bad investments. Then, when it looked like your uncle was going to lose everything, including the villa, Molitor told him he knew a way out."

"Counterfeiting," Doug said.

"Right," Joe said. He took up the story. "Molitor was in a great position to make counterfeit money. He owned a small, private printing plant, and with his connections in the art world he was able to get any kind of special paper without making people suspicious. We may never know who engraved the original plates for him. But when they somehow got damaged, he brought them to the finest engraver he knew— Jacques Dombray."

"My uncle was not a crook," Catherine said fiercely.

"No," Frank replied. "But when his best friend told him that his life was in danger unless the plates were fixed, he agreed to work on them. Then after they were done, he had second thoughts. He hid the completed plates and sent word that he would destroy them unless the counterfeiting gang left Molitor alone. He still thought he was helping a friend in trouble, you see."

"And before he could tell Molitor where the plates were, he died of a heart attack," Joe said. "All Molitor knew was that the plates were somewhere here at the villa, and that their location was somehow connected to the Almanarre Cup."

William came in from the kitchen with a plate of cookies and a big pot of cocoa. Once they were all back in their seats, Doug said, "So Emil was behind the jinx the whole time."

"He had a lot of help from his two accomplices," said Frank. "I actually saw him giving

146

them their orders, the first day we were here, but I had no idea what I was looking at."

"Then what tipped you off?" Ian asked.

"A lot of little things. For instance, those falling tiles. They were rigged that way to give somebody an alibi, and the only people who *had* an alibi were the two roofers. And then there was the portrait that vanished. Only two people could have taken it from the studio—Catherine and Emil Molitor. It didn't seem that important at first, but once I realized that the face in the portrait was the same face that appeared on the counterfeit bank notes, the pieces started to fall into place."

Joe said, "Then there was the way Molitor kept trying to convince everyone that the Villa Dombray was jinxed. If he was such a good friend of Catherine's, why would he want to scare away her guests and ruin her business? It didn't add up."

"I get it," said Doug. "He wanted the place to himself, so he could look for the hidden plates. And his accomplices kept searching people's rooms and created the idea of a jinx. Was it Molitor and his guys who broke Catherine's vases, and tampered with our boards, and set the fire?"

Frank nodded. "He must have been getting pretty frantic, too. He'd used up practically all of his phony bills—some of the last of them turned up in a loan he made to Catherine—and he needed money fast to keep paying the members of his gang. Without those plates, he was finished."

Ian put down his cup and said, "I still don't understand why he stole the Cup. What connection could there be between a windsurfing trophy and a set of counterfeit plates?"

"We don't know," Joe confessed. "But there must be one. Why don't we take a look? Doug, do you mind? The Cup's yours now."

Doug grinned. "With everything that's happened since, I'd almost forgotten that!" He went into Catherine's office and returned with the gleaming silver trophy. They all moved in close as he set it on the table.

"That's an amazing view of Almanarre Bay," Joe said. "You can even make out the individual villas. Catherine," he added suddenly, "do you have a magnifying glass?"

"Of course. There is one in my desk."

She returned in a moment and handed it to him. Joe leaned over until his face was just inches from the Cup. Then he straightened up with a big smile on his face.

"Take a close look at the Villa Dombray," he told Catherine, handing back the magnifying glass. "Do you see a tiny star in the garden, just under one of the windows?"

"But why . . . *Yes!* Yes, of course!"

Joe looked around at the others. "Anybody like

to bet that we won't find the plates buried there?" he demanded. Nobody took him up on it.

"Now that all the mysteries have been explained," Doug said, "I have an announcement to make. Catherine and I have been talking things over, and we've decided that the Almanarre Cup is going to stay right here at Almanarre. And the Villa Dombray is going to be the new headquarters of the Newman School of Windsurfing. To celebrate, tomorrow we're going to throw that beach party that was supposed to happen today."

As everyone cheered, he turned to Joe and Frank. "We owe you guys," he said. "The least we can do is offer you free room, board, and windsurfing lessons for the rest of your lives!"

The Hardys grinned. "Great!" said Frank.

Joe nodded in agreement. "Now *there's* a reward that isn't all wet!"

# THE HARDY BOYS® SERIES
## By Franklin W. Dixon

| | | |
|---|---|---|
| NIGHT OF THE WEREWOLF—#59 | 62480 | $3.50 |
| MYSTERY OF THE SAMURAI SWORD—#60 | 67302 | $3.50 |
| THE PENTAGON SPY—#61 | 67221 | $3.50 |
| THE APEMAN'S SECRET—#62 | 62479 | $3.50 |
| THE MUMMY CASE—#63 | 64289 | $3.50 |
| MYSTERY OF SMUGGLERS COVE—#64 | 66229 | $3.50 |
| THE STONE IDOL—#65 | 62626 | $3.50 |
| THE VANISHING THIEVES—#66 | 63890 | $3.50 |
| THE OUTLAW'S SILVER—#67 | 64285 | $3.50 |
| THE FOUR-HEADED DRAGON—#69 | 65797 | $3.50 |
| THE INFINITY CLUE—#70 | 62475 | $3.50 |
| TRACK OF THE ZOMBIE—#71 | 62623 | $3.50 |
| THE VOODOO PLOT—#72 | 64287 | $3.50 |
| THE BILLION DOLLAR RANSOM—#73 | 66228 | $3.50 |
| TIC-TAC-TERROR—#74 | 66858 | $3.50 |
| TRAPPED AT SEA—#75 | 64290 | $3.50 |
| GAME PLAN FOR DISASTER—#76 | 64288 | $3.50 |
| THE CRIMSON FLAME—#77 | 64286 | $3.50 |
| SKY SABOTAGE—#79 | 62625 | $3.50 |
| THE ROARING RIVER MYSTERY—#80 | 63823 | $3.50 |
| THE DEMON'S DEN—#81 | 62622 | $3.50 |
| THE BLACKWING PUZZLE—#82 | 62624 | $3.50 |
| THE SWAMP MONSTER—#83 | 49727 | $3.50 |
| REVENGE OF THE DESERT PHANTOM—#84 | 49729 | $3.50 |
| SKYFIRE PUZZLE—#85 | 67458 | $3.50 |
| THE MYSTERY OF THE SILVER STAR—#86 | 64374 | $3.50 |
| PROGRAM FOR DESTRUCTION—#87 | 64895 | $3.50 |
| TRICKY BUSINESS—#88 | 64973 | $3.50 |
| THE SKY BLUE FRAME—#89 | 64974 | $3.50 |
| DANGER ON THE DIAMOND—#90 | 63425 | $3.50 |
| SHIELD OF FEAR—#91 | 66308 | $3.50 |
| THE SHADOW KILLERS—#92 | 66309 | $3.50 |
| THE BILLION DOLLAR RANSOM—#93 | 66310 | $3.50 |
| BREAKDOWN IN AXEBLADE—#94 | 66311 | $3.50 |
| DANGER ON THE AIR—#95 | 66305 | $3.50 |
| WIPEOUT—#96 | 66306 | $3.50 |
| THE HARDY BOYS® GHOST STORIES | 50808 | $3.50 |
| NANCY DREW® AND THE HARDY BOYS® SUPER SLEUTHS | 43375 | $3.50 |
| NANCY DREW® AND THE HARDY BOYS® SUPER SLEUTHS #2 | 50194 | $3.50 |

NANCY DREW® and THE HARDY BOYS® are trademarks of Simon & Schuster,
registered in the United States Patent and Trademark Office.

**AND DON'T FORGET...NANCY DREW CASEFILES® NOW AVAILABLE IN PAPERBACK.**